FINDING OUT
THE TERRIBLE TRUTH

Melanie looked at the pile of letters in her lap. She wanted to go on reading them. There was something almost magic in holding them in her hands and knowing that they had been sent to someone very much like herself so long ago. She could almost see Cordia's flirtatious smile as she bestowed it on first one young man and then another.

"I know just how she felt," Melanie murmured.

She retied the letters with the pink bow and then noticed another letter. Her own mother's return address was in the corner. What caught her eye was the postmark, which was only seven months before her own birth, and a notation on the envelope: "News That Kathy's Going to Have a Baby."

Melanie stared at the letter for a moment. Kathy was her mother's name. It gave her a tingly feeling to see the letter lying there and know it was about her before she was even born.

Should I read it, or shouldn't I? she wondered.

"It's about me," Melanie said aloud. "So I'm going to read it. . . ."

Bantam Skylark Books by Betsy Haynes
Ask your bookseller for the books you have missed

THE AGAINST TAFFY SINCLAIR CLUB
TAFFY SINCLAIR STRIKES AGAIN
TAFFY SINCLAIR, QUEEN OF THE SOAPS
TAFFY SINCLAIR AND THE ROMANCE
  MACHINE DISASTER
BLACKMAILED BY TAFFY SINCLAIR
TAFFY SINCLAIR, BABY ASHLEY, AND ME
TAFFY SINCLAIR AND THE SECRET ADMIRER
  EPIDEMIC
TAFFY SINCLAIR AND THE MELANIE MAKE-OVER
THE TRUTH ABOUT TAFFY SINCLAIR
THE GREAT MOM SWAP
THE GREAT BOYFRIEND TRAP

Books in The Fabulous Five Series

1 SEVENTH-GRADE RUMORS
2 THE TROUBLE WITH FLIRTING
3 THE POPULARITY TRAP
4 HER HONOR, KATIE SHANNON
5 THE BRAGGING WAR
6 THE PARENT GAME
7 THE KISSING DISASTER
8 THE RUNAWAY CRISIS
9 THE BOYFRIEND DILEMMA
#10 PLAYING THE PART
#11 HIT AND RUN
#12 KATIE'S DATING TIPS
#13 THE CHRISTMAS COUNTDOWN
#14 SEVENTH-GRADE MENACE
#15 MELANIE'S IDENTITY CRISIS

THE FABULOUS FIVE

Melanie's Identity Crisis

BETSY HAYNES

A BANTAM SKYLARK BOOK®
NEW YORK · TORONTO · LONDON · SYDNEY · AUCKLAND

RL 5, IL age 9—12

MELANIE'S IDENTITY CRISIS
A Bantam Skylark Book / February 1990

ISBN 0-553-15775-2

Published simultaneously in the United States and Canada

PRINTED IN THE UNITED STATES OF AMERICA

CWO   0 9 8 7 6 5 4 3 2 1

Melanie's Identity Crisis

CHAPTER

1

"Eek! I'm having an identity crisis!" squealed Melanie Edwards. She held her ballpoint pen by two fingers and let it drop like a bomb onto the open notebook in her lap as she looked helplessly at her friends. "I can't answer all these questions about myself."

"Maybe I can help you," Katie Shannon said with a grin. "Name: Melanie Edwards. Favorite sport: flirting with boys. Favorite indoor activity: thinking about boys. Favorite outdoor activity: looking at boys. Favorite subject: studying boys."

"*Shhh!*" Melanie said quickly, looking around the crowded gymnasium where most of the Wakeman

Junior High students were spending a rainy lunch period after leaving the cafeteria. "Someone might hear you and think I'm boy crazy."

"Don't worry. Everybody already knows," said Beth Barry with a laugh, and then she ducked as Melanie pretended to throw a book at her.

"I agree with Melanie about the questionnaire," admitted Jana Morgan. "It's hard. I don't know my library card number, and I'm not sure about some of the other things either, especially the questions about my favorites."

"But remember what Mrs. Blankenship said in Family Living class," Christie Winchell reminded them. "Answering these questions will help us know ourselves a little better before we begin looking for our ancestors in the genealogy project." Then she added, "I think it's going to be fun. I've always wondered if there were any skeletons in the old family closet."

Beth's eyes gleamed. "Yeah. Murderers. Pirates. Bank robbers."

Melanie nodded to Christie. "Mrs. Clark said the same thing in our class. She also said that if we traced our families only as far back as 1625, we'd find over *sixteen thousand* people directly related to us, and that's only parents and grandparents. It doesn't count brothers and sisters or aunts and uncles."

"Wow. I wonder how many great-great-greats that is?" asked Beth.

"I don't know," said Melanie. "But I thought it was neat when she said that we're all unique because each one of our ancestors contributed a little bit of themselves in the genes they passed on to us, and that's why we're all so different from each other."

"Different, but still best friends," Jana said emphatically. "No matter what, we'll always be The Fabulous Five."

Everybody agreed with that, then went back to working on the questionnaires. Melanie tried to concentrate on the next two questions—*Favorite food? Food you dislike most?*—but instead she glanced at the groups of kids milling around in the gym while thunder crashed outside and rain streamed down the windows. Some sat in the bleachers just as she and her friends were doing. Others stood beside the big double doors leading into the hall or near the rest rooms. Mostly the girls were talking quietly, and lots of the boys were horsing around, but just as the Family Living teachers had said, no two were alike. Unless you counted the Dalworth twins, of course, thought Melanie. Mike and Mitch were so much alike that even their teachers couldn't tell them apart, but they were identical twins and shared the same genes.

When the bell rang, Melanie headed for her afternoon classes, promising the others that she would meet them after school to go to Bumpers, the fast-food restaurant where the junior high kids hung out. As she walked through the halls, she thought about what Jana had said about The Fabulous Five. They certainly were all different. Jana was the unofficial leader, the one who could hold everything together in a crisis. Christie was the studious one and the math brain. Katie was the feminist and the person who worried most about things being fair. Beth was the actress who did everything with dramatic flair. And of course, everybody always says that I'm boy crazy, Melanie thought, when the truth is that I'm just *interested* in boys.

Thinking of boys reminded her that if she speeded up a little and turned the next corner at the right instant, she might just meet Garrett Boldt heading in her direction. She usually only managed to get her timing right once or twice a week, but Garrett was so totally handsome and terrific that she almost slid around the corner in anticipation of seeing him.

"Hi, Garrett," she yelled when his head appeared above the crowd. He was in the eighth grade and one of the tallest boys in Wakeman, which made him easy to spot. She bounced on her tiptoes and tried to get his attention with a wave. "Gar-*rett*!" she called insistently. "Hey, Flash," she added, using the nickname he had earned as sports photographer for the school yearbook, *The Wigwam*.

But Garrett moved on past her, looking straight ahead. The crowd was moving too fast in each direction for her to have time to call out again. He hadn't heard her, and yet she felt sure she had yelled loud enough. Could he have been ignoring me? she wondered.

When she got to her seat in biology class, the first thing she did was look for Shane Arrington. Shane was one of her major crushes along with Scott Daly, her old boyfriend from Mark Twain Elementary. Shane liked her, too. Well enough, anyway, to ask her out now and then and kiss her good-night when he brought her home. And he was *soooo* handsome, a dead ringer for River Phoenix.

"Hmmm," she murmured to herself as she watched him walk in the door. "I wonder what my Family Living teacher would say about that. They can't possibly have the same genes."

She had planned to wait for Shane to walk by her desk so that she could ambush him with a flirty smile. Then she would start a conversation by asking him if he had found a girlfriend yet for Igor, his pet iguana, whom he claimed had been so lovesick that he hadn't eaten for days. But Shane stopped to talk to Shawnie Pendergast, and an instant later Mr. Dracovitch called the class to order.

Rats! One perfectly good ambush down the drain, she thought as she watched Shane slide into his seat without looking in her direction.

Melanie slumped in her seat and halfheartedly listened to the biology teacher begin the lesson. Nothing was going her way today. Garrett had passed her in the hall without noticing her. Shane had talked to Shawnie instead of her, and this morning before school, Scott Daly had streaked by her on his bicycle without even saying hello.

She sagged a little lower in her desk as she thought about the three boys. Scott is my very best boyfriend. But Shane is too cute for words, and he's so kooky. Who else would have an iguana for a pet? And Garrett Boldt is dreamy. So what if he's an eighth-grader and popular? He likes me a little bit. At least I thought he did. What's the matter with all three of them, anyway? They're acting as if I don't exist!

Melanie sighed so loudly that three students turned around to look at her. Fortunately, Mr. Dracovitch had his back to the class writing on the board, and he didn't notice.

Mrs. Clark was so revved up over the genealogy project that Melanie thought she was acting almost hyper when she called the Family Living class to order the last period of the day.

"Boys and girls, I'm so excited about the things

we're going to do over the next few weeks that I can hardly wait to get started." She raked her fingers through her short, salt-and-pepper hair as she paced up and down at the front of the room. "Maybe some of you will find out that you're related to someone famous or that your ancestors came over on the *Mayflower*. Wouldn't that be fun?"

Some kids nodded and a few even cheered.

"But before we begin our detective work," she went on, holding up a sample of the questionnaire she had given to each student, "we still have some work to do. Now, who can tell me what they learned about themselves from filling out one of these?"

"That I don't like to fill out questionnaires," blurted out Joel Murphy.

Mrs. Clark gave him a tolerant nod. "And?" she said, trying to coax something more out of Joel.

Joel shrugged, and Mrs. Clark looked around the class for another volunteer.

Melanie ducked her head behind Tony Calcaterra's to avoid being called on. She had only answered half of the questions. I already know everything there is to know about myself, she thought grumpily. It was boys she wanted to know more about. Maybe Mrs. Clark ought to collect everybody's questionnaire and then put all the ones the boys turned in into a book that she could run off on the copy machine and give to any girl who wanted it.

What a great idea! she thought. The list of things she would like to know about certain boys was practically endless.

There were other people she wanted to know about, too. What made Laura McCall so snooty? Or why did Katie Shannon have such opposite opinions from hers about boys? And what made Christie Winchell and Whitney Larkin extra smart? But still, she thought, it was boys she was the most interested in finding out about.

Across the room, Kim Baxter was waving her hand in the air, and Melanie turned her attention back to what was going on in class.

"Yes, Kim. What did you find out about yourself?" asked Mrs. Clark.

"Well, this isn't on the questionnaire, but my mom reminded me that I'm the only one in our family who has red hair."

Clarence Marshall snickered loudly, and Mrs. Clark gave him a warning frown before saying, "Isn't that interesting, Kim? I'll bet when you begin searching, you'll find that one of your ancestors had the same color hair as you."

"My older brother throws up every time he eats fish," offered a boy at the back of the room whom Melanie knew only as Tom something-or-other.

This time the whole class broke out laughing.

"Now, class!" said Mrs. Clark sternly. "I hope that

you have all used these questionnaires about your-
selves to see that we all have specific traits that make
us different from each other and that those traits can
sometimes be traced to our ancestors. Now it is time
for us to become detectives and begin digging up our
ancestors. We're going to start looking for clues to
why we are certain ways and who was responsible
for our being that way. In order to do that, I am
going to give each one of you genealogy charts to
trace your own family tree."

The laughter turned to groans as she passed stacks
of papers down each row.

"More paperwork," muttered Curtis.

Mrs. Clark nodded. "That's right. But you'll see.
It's going to be fun."

Melanie perked up as she looked at the chart in
her hand. It really was a family tree just as Mrs.
Clark had said. The main trunk coming up from the
ground contained space for her own name, date of
birth, and place of birth. Two branches grew out of
the trunk. On one of them it said *Mother's name*, and
that was followed by spaces for her date and place of
birth, whom she married, and for use in the future,
when she died and where she was buried. The same
information was asked for on her father's branch. On
each parent's branch were two branches for their
parents, and so on until the top of the tree contained
dozens of small branches for more distant relatives.

"Cool," murmured Tony Calcaterra from the seat in front of her.

Melanie had to agree. It was going to be fun to fill in all those blanks.

"For tomorrow's assignment, I want you to talk to your parents and fill in as much information as you can on your family tree. Once you've listed everything your mother and father can tell you, I'll teach you the next place that family detectives always go to find clues."

Melanie glanced at her family tree again. I wonder what I'll find out when I start digging into our family's history? she mused. Maybe I'm related to a famous person, just as Mrs. Clark suggested someone might be. Or maybe I'll trace our ancestors back to royalty.

"Princess Melanie," she whispered, and giggled softly. Whatever it turned out to be, it was going to be fun.

CHAPTER

2

*B*umpers was packed by the time Melanie and her friends got there after school. They made their way through the maze of booths, tables, and bumper cars that were relics from an old amusement park and gave the place its name, looking for some place to sit. Finally Katie spotted an empty table near the back and led them to it. All around them kids were talking about the genealogy project and tracing their family trees.

"Well, at least I understand Brittany now," said Beth emphatically.

"Your older sister?" asked Christie. "What does she have to do with tracing your family tree?"

"She's so weird that I always felt sure we weren't related," Beth said with a grin. "You know, that when Mom brought Brittany home from the hospital, she had the wrong baby. Now I know that we just inherited genes from different ancestors. What a relief!"

Everyone giggled.

"I was thinking about Mr. Dracovitch," admitted Katie. "Talk about scrambled genes. Can you imagine what kind of relatives it took to produce him? Maybe he really is a descendant of Count Dracula. Otherwise, why would a grown man wear a shiny black toupee that makes him look like Dracula and cook garbage on a Bunsen burner in his classroom?"

"If you ask me, he's pretty neat," said Christie. "I think it's his way of saying that it's okay to be different."

The next morning Melanie joined the group of boys and girls standing in The Fabulous Five's regular spot by the school fence just in time to hear Tony Calcaterra say, "I hope I find out that I'm related to Sylvester Stallone. You know, the Italian Stallion." He flexed his muscles and strutted around imitating the actor. "You guys will have to admit that there's a definite family resemblance."

"Yeah, two eyes, two ears, two feet. There's a family resemblance, all right," Katie scoffed good-naturedly. "Don't get big ideas just because you are Italian and have black hair."

"The way I see it, I'm bound to find the answer to all the questions about UFOs," bragged Shane, waving his arms toward the heavens.

"Unidentified flying objects?" asked Christie, making a face. "Why?"

"Hey, my parents had to come from another planet. Right? They're so far out that there's no other explanation."

"Man, that's cosmic," teased Beth, making a peace sign. Then she turned to Jana and said, "And maybe you'll discover that you really are related to Trevor Morgan after all and that you can get all of us front-row tickets for Brain Damage's concerts."

Jana raised an eyebrow at her friend. "Dream on," she said. "Imagine me and a rock star related."

Melanie listened to them talk, but she didn't join in the conversation. How could she when Shane was ignoring her again? She didn't even feel like asking him about Igor.

What's wrong with me? she wondered. Have I suddenly become invisible?

Melanie looked over her genealogy chart while she waited for Family Living class to start later that day. She had shown the family tree to her parents after dinner the night before and had asked them to tell her everything they knew about her ancestors so she could fill in all the spaces.

"Well, you got your brains from your mother's side and your good looks from my side," joked her father.

"Come on, Larry," her mother chided. "This is serious." Then her eyes twinkled and she added, "Besides, she got *both* her brains and her good looks from my side."

Melanie loved it when her parents joked like that. It made her feel so warm and specially loved. She smiled at both of them and then said, "I know Grandma and Grandpa Pennington and Grandma and Grandpa Edwards, but I don't know when they were born or married or any of that other stuff, and I don't even remember the names of their parents."

For the next hour and a half the three of them sat around the kitchen table, filling in spaces on the family tree until Mrs. Edwards had traced her mother's family all the way back to Melanie's great-great-grandmother Cordia Mae Lee, who had been born in 1896.

"Wow," said Melanie. "That was almost one hundred years ago."

"And from what I've heard, she was really a character," her mother said, and chuckled.

"In your family, everyone's a character," said Mr. Edwards, teasing again. "Now in *my* family everybody has always been serious, and hardworking, and the sort of people who stayed out of mischief."

They had laughed hard over that, and the warm feeling had washed over Melanie again. Still, she wanted to know more.

"Tell me about Great-great-grandmother Cordia," Melanie insisted. "What do you mean, she was a character?"

Her mother was thoughtful for a moment. "Well, I don't really know very much about her. I've just always heard stories from my mother and grandmother about how she was always getting into mischief when she was young, especially where boys were concerned."

"Boys?" Melanie whispered as little tingles traveled up her spine.

"That's right," said her mother. "According to the stories, she had so many boyfriends that her girlfriends were jealous."

But that was all her mother had been able to tell her about Great-great-grandmother Cordia, and now, sitting in class and looking at the chart with over half of the blanks filled in, Melanie was curious again about the ancestor who had gotten into mischief because of boys. She couldn't help remembering Mrs. Clark's words: "What you are is partly because of your ancestors, who each contributed a little bit of themselves in the form of the genes they passed on to you. You are all of them, and you are like no one else. You are *yourself*." What had her great-great-grandmother really been like? she wondered. And had some of Cordia Mae Lee's personality been passed on down to her?

Just then Mrs. Clark came bustling into the room. "Good afternoon, class," she called. "How many of you filled in at least part of your family trees? Let me see hands."

Hands shot up all over the room. In fact, as she glanced around, Melanie could only see two kids who had not raised theirs, Funny Hawthorne and Joel Murphy. Joel was late handing in his homework half the time, she mused, so it wasn't strange that he hadn't filled in his family tree. But why hadn't Funny?

Melanie looked closely at her. Funny's usually smiling face was serious now and her eyes were downcast. That's strange, thought Melanie. Jana had told her that Funny's real name was Karen Janelle Hawthorne, but her family had nicknamed her Funny because of her sunny disposition. She had liked to laugh so much when she was a baby that they had started calling her Funny, and the name had stuck. Melanie couldn't remember ever seeing her before without a smile on her face.

"Good," said Mrs. Clark. "I'm glad so many of you have gotten started because the next thing you're going to do is get to know the relatives on your charts."

Melanie blinked in surprise. Had her teacher been reading her mind about her great-great-grandmother? But how could she possibly get to know someone who had been born and died years ago?

Across the room Clarence Marshall asked almost the same question. "How can we get to know someone who's dead?"

"That's a very good question, Clarence," said Mrs. Clark. "We're going to do what other good detectives do, ask questions."

A few kids giggled, and someone whispered loudly, "But if they're dead, how are they going to answer?"

"I heard that," Mrs. Clark called out good-naturedly. "The answer is, you're going to talk to the people in your family who are still alive and ask them to tell you any stories they know about the ancestors on your chart. You can ask your parents or your aunts and uncles or even your grandparents or great-grandparents, if they're still alive. In fact, sometimes it's more fun to talk to older relatives because they can remember people and things that no one else in the family even knows about."

For the next few minutes Mrs. Clark gave them suggestions for ways to talk to their relatives about the ancestors who especially interested them, and

Melanie began to make plans to find out about Great-great-grandmother Cordia. Had her girl-friends accused her of being boy crazy? Melanie wondered, feeling instant sympathy for this relative who had lived so long ago. If they did, I certainly know how she felt, Melanie thought. It was going to be fun to find out about her. Maybe she would even be able to find out something about the boys Cordia had liked. Wouldn't it be weird if any of them were named Scott or Shane or Garrett? she thought, and almost giggled out loud.

But who should she talk to first about Great-great-grandmother Cordia? Her mother had told her all that she knew about her illustrious ancestor. Maybe she should ask her own grandmother if she knew any stories.

When the bell rang ending classes for the day, Melanie headed for her locker. Seeing Funny Hawthorne ahead of her, she called, "Hey, Funny. Wait up."

Funny glanced over her shoulder and slowed up when she saw Melanie, but she didn't stop to wait. And she still wasn't smiling.

Melanie surged forward to catch her, wondering what had Funny so upset. They were friends, but not best friends because Funny belonged to a rival clique called The Fantastic Foursome, so she couldn't just ask Funny what was wrong. Maybe she should just talk about school and give Funny a chance to tell her what was troubling her on her own, if she felt like it.

"Isn't the genealogy project fun?" Melanie began, remembering too late that Funny hadn't filled out any of her family tree.

"I don't see anything fun about it," grumbled Funny. "If you ask me, it's dumb."

"Oh, you won't think so once you get started," Melanie assured her. "I found out that I had this great-great-grandmother who was always getting into trouble with her friends because she was boy crazy. Isn't that wild? I can hardly wait to find out more about her and some of the others, too. Maybe then I'll understand myself better."

"Big deal," muttered Funny.

"But Funny," Melanie insisted, surprised at Funny's reaction. "You've probably got some pretty interesting relatives, too. You ought to at least find out who they are."

Funny stopped beside the table where the hall monitor sat during classtime and slammed her notebook down on it. Glaring at Melanie, she opened the notebook and pulled out a sheet of paper that she held up for Melanie to see.

"It's your genealogy chart, and it's blank," said Melanie. "So why are you showing it to me?"

Without answering, Funny began tearing the paper in half. After she ripped it down the middle, she put the two pieces together and tore them in half, too. Next, she tore those pieces into dozens of tiny pieces and threw them into the air like confetti. Then she stomped off down the hall, leaving Melanie staring after her.

CHAPTER

3

*M*elanie stood helpless for a moment, watching the bits of paper drift downward like snowflakes and wondering what to do. Obviously Funny was upset over the genealogy project, and it was just as obvious that she didn't want to talk about why. But still, Melanie reasoned, at a time like this, Funny needed a friend, and none of her Fantastic Foursome friends were anywhere to be seen.

Melanie gave one last glance around as Funny ducked into the girls' room at the far end of the hallway. The crowd was already thinning as kids went to their lockers and then headed for home. Or for Bumpers, she thought. She had told her friends she would meet them there. I'll still make it to Bumpers right after I talk to Funny, she assured herself as she hurried down the hall and pushed open the bathroom door.

Funny was standing by one of the sinks, staring at the water faucet, but no water was coming out. Melanie let the door close behind her and stood there without saying anything for a moment, hoping Funny would look up and start the conversation herself. She didn't.

Finally Melanie took a deep breath and said, "I'm sorry if I said something that upset you. I didn't mean to. Honest."

Funny shook her head and then raised her eyes to look at Melanie in the mirror. "It wasn't your fault." She shrugged apologetically. "It's the genealogy project. I just don't want to do it, that's all."

Now it was Melanie's turn to look down. She didn't know how to respond to Funny. She had already mentioned how much fun it was going to be to learn about their ancestors and find out more about themselves, and that had made Funny angry. What more was there to say?

"It's because . . ." Funny's voice trailed off so that Melanie couldn't hear the reason she gave.

"What did you say?"

Funny fidgeted from one foot to the other and chewed her lower lip. "I *said*"—she paused, sighing deeply—"it's because I'm adopted. I don't know much about my birth family, and what good will it do to find out about the Hawthorne ancestors? I'm not like any of them anyway. Some family tree, huh?" she grumbled.

Melanie looked away from Funny, trying to hide her embarrassment and fumbling for something to say.

"Oh, it's okay," said Funny. "I've just never told anybody. The Hawthornes adopted me when I was a tiny baby, and I forget about it myself most of the time. But now that Mrs. Clark has started this stupid project, I don't know what to do."

"Have you talked to your parents about it?" asked Melanie. Then she winced, wondering if the word "parents" had been the right choice.

"No," said Funny. "I was afraid that if I brought up the subject, they'd think I wanted to know about all that other stuff, and it might hurt their feelings. We're pretty close, and I'd die if they got the wrong idea. They might think I didn't love them."

Melanie nodded. She could appreciate Funny's feeling that way. She remembered the warm glow she had gotten the night before when she had been joking with her mother and father about which one of them had given her good looks and which one brains. It would be awful if they ever thought she cared about someone else.

"I know I could just go ahead and fill out the family tree with my Hawthorne family just to get a good grade in Family Living," Funny went on. "But this genealogy project is making my life just too confusing. Instead of finding out who I am, the way Mrs. Clark said we would, I'm starting to feel like a nobody. I don't really belong to anyone."

Melanie's eyes widened and she rushed to Funny. "Oh, no. You can't feel that way! You're a super person. Everybody likes you because you smile all the time and cheer people up. Don't say you feel like a nobody."

Funny looked startled for an instant, then seemed to smile in spite of herself. "Thanks," she said, giving Melanie's hand a warm squeeze. Glancing quickly at her watch, she added, "Eeek! I'd better get out of here. My friends will be wondering what happened to me."

"Mine, too," agreed Melanie.

The girls said good-bye and went to their lockers, and as they turned in different directions in the hall, Melanie called out to Funny that she would see her at Bumpers. But when Melanie arrived a little while later and spotted Laura McCall, Tammy Lucero, and Melissa McConnell sitting on stools at the counter, Funny wasn't with them. She's feeling better so she'll be here, Melanie told herself, but even though she kept an eye on the door, Funny never arrived. I guess she wasn't feeling that much better after all, Melanie told herself.

As she walked home a little while later, Melanie thought about Funny's predicament and sympathized with her all over again. Funny had said that she felt like a nobody. It must be *awful* to feel that way, she mused.

CHAPTER

4

Shane caught up with Melanie a block from school the next morning. He was puffing and panting as if he had run all the way from home.

"Hey, what's up?" she asked as he slowed beside her. "You usually beat me to school by at least fifteen minutes."

He looked worried as he shook his head. "It's Igor. I've been holding his claw most of the night. Finally the sun came up and he dropped off to sleep."

"Is he still pining away for a girlfriend?" she asked, trying her best to swallow the giggle that was bubbling up in her throat. She didn't want Shane to know that she burst out laughing every time she thought about a lovesick iguana.

"Yeah," said Shane. "We thought we had it figured out. The pet shop at the mall said we could put him in the pen with their iguanas if we promised to buy whichever one he took an interest in, and we were sure he'd find someone he could relate to there." He gave Melanie a quick look. "Iguanas are sensitive, you know. Just any girlfriend won't do."

"Really?" asked Melanie.

Shane nodded. "Anyway, we put his collar with his identification tags on him and took him out there as soon as my folks got home from work yesterday, but it was a disaster."

"A disaster?" Melanie echoed. "Weren't there any girl iguanas at the pet shop?"

"Oh, there were plenty of girls," Shane assured her. "That wasn't the trouble. There were plenty of boy iguanas, too, and they jumped on poor Igor the minute he started getting friendly with one of the girls. It's a good thing we didn't just drop him off and head back home. If we hadn't hung around a few minutes and been there to rescue him, he might have been killed."

"Wow. Is he okay?"

Shane nodded again. "He's okay, but he's really in a blue funk."

Melanie gave Shane a sympathetic look. "I can certainly see why he'd be depressed," she said.

By now they had reached the school ground, and Shane waved good-bye and peeled off toward a group of boys congregated near the baseball diamond. Melanie watched him go, shaking her head. Sometimes she wasn't sure just how seriously to take the things he said. And she couldn't help feeling a catch in her throat when she thought that all he seemed to want to talk to her about was Igor.

"Why are you standing over here all by yourself?" Melanie was startled by Beth's words. She blinked and looked at her friend, who was bounding toward her from the direction of the rest of The Fabulous Five.

"Don't tell me you have amnesia and don't remember your name, who your best friends are, or where you stand every morning before school," Beth quipped.

Melanie gave her a sheepish grin. "No, I was just talking to Shane. You wouldn't believe what he told me about his latest attempts to find a girlfriend for Igor." Melanie repeated Shane's story for Beth, and they both had a good laugh. "Come on," said Melanie. "I just remembered my name, who my best friends are, and where I always stand before school every morning."

When they reached their usual spot by the fence, which was becoming a gathering place for more than just The Fabulous Five, Joel Murphy was talking.

". . . so that's why I need an extra copy of the family tree."

"I missed that," said Melanie. "Why do you need an extra copy of the family tree? Did somebody chop yours down?" she added, and then laughed at her own joke.

Joel rolled his eyes toward the sky. "Get serious," he said. "I need two copies because I have two fathers, my real dad and my stepdad. I can't get all those names on one sheet."

"Joel, that's silly," insisted Jana. "You only need to trace the family you're related to. I have a father and a stepfather, too, and that's what I'm doing. You didn't get any genes from your stepdad."

Joel looked at Jana out of the corner of his eye and then shrugged. "I thought if I turned in two, maybe I'd get a better grade."

Just then the first bell rang, and Melanie headed for her locker. What Jana had said about herself and Joel's not being related to their stepfathers made her think about Funny again. Poor Funny. She didn't have any choice about which family she would trace. It would have to be the Hawthornes. And when she did, she still wouldn't know anything about herself. It was no wonder she felt like a nobody.

Melanie thought about Funny a lot during the morning, and by the time lunch period arrived and The Fabulous Five were sitting at their table in the cafeteria out of earshot of anyone else, she had decided to talk to them about Funny's predicament. She would ask them to keep it a secret because she didn't want to betray Funny's confidence. But just the same, she felt that Funny needed help, more help than she could give her alone.

"Gosh, I didn't know she was adopted," said Christie when Melanie had finished telling them the story. "I feel sorry for her."

"I don't," piped up Katie. The others gave her strange looks and she added, "Not because she's adopted anyway. Lots of people are. It's no big deal. I only feel sorry for her if she's having trouble handling it."

"I didn't know she was adopted either," said Jana. "But it wouldn't have made any difference in how much I like her. I'll have to admit, though, I thought she had been acting strangely for the past couple of days. She's usually so bouncy and full of fun, but now that you mention it, she's been awfully quiet lately."

Melanie sighed. "Since she confided in me, I feel as if I ought to be able to give her some good advice, but I can't. I don't know any more about what she should do than she does."

"Do you know what I think?" asked Katie in a voice that made the others put down their sandwiches and look at her. "I think she should definitely talk to her parents. I mean, after all, they're . . . well, they're her *parents*. I'm sure they're prepared for her to have questions about herself, and they've probably got some answers ready for her."

"You're right," agreed Melanie, and the others nodded. "It's really the only thing that makes sense. If anyone can help her, they can."

"I agree," said Christie. "I'd go to my parents if I was worried about something like that."

Melanie felt better. Since Funny was in her Family Living class the last period of the day, she could talk to her then. She could get to the classroom early and wait outside the door until Funny showed up. She'd figure out exactly what to say when the time came.

CHAPTER

5

"*H*i, Funny. Can I talk to you a minute?" Melanie called as she saw Funny coming toward the Family Living classroom.

Funny's expression was still uncharacteristically sober, but she brightened a little when she saw Melanie. "Hi, Mel," she said, smiling faintly and heading in Melanie's direction.

Melanie cleared her throat nervously. She still hadn't figured out exactly the right words to use. "I've been thinking about your genealogy project. You know . . . why you don't want to do it," she began.

Funny looked at her sharply, and Melanie went on

before she could lose her nerve. "I think you should talk to your parents. Maybe you could just show them the chart, explain the project, and let them take it from there. They're smart. They'll know what you're thinking, and they'll understand how you feel. After all, they love you, don't they?"

"But that's just the point," Funny insisted. "It might make *them* feel bad."

"Maybe. But maybe not, too. They've known since they adopted you that someday something like this might come up."

Funny sighed. "I know you're right," she said. "It's just that it's going to be hard."

Melanie reached out and gave Funny's hand a warm squeeze. "Tell you what," she said brightly. "I'll keep my fingers crossed for you. And my toes! And my ears! And my eyes!" At that she crossed her eyes and made a goofy face, which sent Funny into peals of laughter.

"Oh, Melanie. You're a terrific friend. I'll talk to them tonight and tell you what I find out in the morning."

Funny was still smiling when the two girls got to class and took their seats. Melanie was pleased to see Funny back to her old self, but she hadn't been kidding her when she said she would keep everything crossed that she possibly could. It would be awful for Funny if her parents did actually get upset.

"Who has found out something interesting?" asked Mrs. Clark once the class had come to order.

Curtis Trowbridge was the first to raise his hand.

"Tell us what you found, Curtis," said Mrs. Clark.

"One of my ancestors, Jonathan Barlowe, was a spy in the Revolutionary War and he's buried in the old cemetery north of town."

A few wows and all rights sounded through the class as Curtis looked around proudly.

"Good detective work," said Mrs. Clark. "I'm sure there are several of you whose families settled in this area many years ago and who have ancestors buried in the old cemetery. Because of that, I have scheduled a special field trip for Friday afternoon. We are going to go to the old cemetery and become grave rubbers."

"Grave robbers!" cried Tony. "That's against the law."

Melanie chuckled, thinking about how Tony probably knew more about the law than anyone else in the class since he had been taken to Teen Court so many times for breaking school rules.

"I didn't say grave *robbers*, Tony," Mrs. Clark corrected. "I said grave *rubbers*. What that means is, we're going to make gravestone rubbings. We'll take heavy wrapping paper, masking tape, and a box of large wax crayons with us. Then we'll find some old gravestones, preferably marking the graves of some of your own ancestors, and we'll tape the paper over the words carved in the stone. Then we'll rub the crayons over the carvings and make our own picture of the gravestone. Now, who can tell me what important information we can get off the gravestones?"

Melanie only half-listened to the other students say things such as names, dates of birth, dates of death, and things like that. She was already thinking about asking her grandmother if Great-great-grandmother Cordia was buried in that cemetery and planning to make a rubbing of her gravestone if she was.

After school, she hurried straight to her grandmother's house without going either to Bumpers or home. Her grandmother, Marounah Lee Phillips Pennington, was a tiny woman who stood less than five feet tall. "Come on in, love," her grandmother called out when Melanie rang the bell and peeked in the back-door window of her neat little brick house just four blocks from the Edwardses.

"Hi, Gran," said Melanie, stepping into Gran Pennington's sunny yellow kitchen where cookies and hot chocolate were waiting on the table. Melanie had called her grandmother the night before and told her about the genealogy project and the kind of information she would be needing.

"I suppose you want to get right to the important

stuff," said her grandmother with a twinkle in her eye. She was loading the plate of cookies onto a tray as she spoke. "Get your cocoa and come on up to the spare bedroom. That's where I keep the trunk with all the old letters and pictures."

Melanie followed the elderly woman into a tidy room and sat down gingerly on an ancient four-poster bed. The lace bedspread was hand-crocheted, and little lace doilies decorated the tall chest of drawers. But the thing that caught Melanie's attention was an old brass-bound trunk with a domed lid, which sat beneath the window.

Gran Pennington saw her look of admiration and said, "That trunk belonged to your great-great-grandmother, Cordia Mae Lee. Now there was someone who was a character." She laughed softly as she put the cookies on the bureau and sat down in a rocking chair.

Melanie's heart skipped a beat. It was almost as if her grandmother had known whom she most wanted to talk about.

"But back to the chest. Before she was married it was her hope chest. Do you know what a hope chest is?"

Melanie took a sip of her cocoa as she thought a moment and then shook her head. She had never heard of such a thing.

"In your great-great-grandmother's day, young

ladies did fancy needlework. They embroidered pillow slips and made lace tablecloths and things of
that sort and put them away in trunks like this so
that when they got married, they would already
have some of the things they would need."

"Neat!" cried Melanie. "I wonder why girls don't
do that now?"

Gran Pennington nodded her head knowingly.
"Well, I expect it's because girls nowadays are too
busy. They can't sit still long enough to embroider
pillow slips."

Melanie started to mention that she had begun
working on a counted cross-stitch picture once, but
of course she had never finished it.

"You said on the telephone that you'd like to ask
me some questions," her grandmother said. "I'm
ready if you are."

Melanie swallowed a mouthful of warm chocolate
chip cookie and opened her notebook. "Okay," she
said, making a number 1 beside the top line. "Tell
me about yourself. When were you born? Where?
When did you get married to Grandpa Pennington?
That sort of stuff."

Dutifully, Gran Pennington recited the information while Melanie wrote it in her notebook. Every
so often the older lady would remember a story
about her childhood or the early days of her marriage, and Melanie would make notes about that,

too, and about Grandpa Pennington, who had died two years ago. Finally they had exhausted the questions about Gran Pennington, and Melanie brought up her great-great-grandmother.

"You said Cordia Mae Lee was a character. Mom said something like that, too. What can you tell me about her? Is she buried in the old cemetery north of town?"

"Yes, she's buried there, and I even have some pictures of her in one of these old albums." Gran Pennington carefully lifted the trunk lid and removed a fragile leather-bound album with PHOTOGRAPHS written across the front in scrolly gold letters. She opened it, turned a few yellowed pages, and smiled. Then she handed the album to Melanie.

"There she is, sitting under a shade tree in front of the old family home. She was very musical. In fact, that's where your mother gets her talent on the piano. You know," she added brightly, "I've never noticed until now just how much the two of you favor each other. You even have Cordia's reddish-brown hair and blue eyes."

Melanie blinked as she looked at the picture. There was Great-great-grandmother Cordia, sitting under a tree with sheets of music spread around her and smiling at the camera. But what gave Melanie such an eerie feeling was that her grandmother had been right about how much she resembled her rela-

tive from long ago. It was almost as if she were looking at herself in a mirror.

"Now let me see, what can I tell you about her?"
said Gran Pennington, rubbing her chin and gazing
thoughtfully into the distance. "As you can see, your
great-great-grandmother was a very pretty young
woman," she began slowly. "So pretty, in fact, that
the young men swarmed around her like bees
around honey."

Tingles raced up Melanie's spine, and she couldn't
help smiling with pleasure. "Really?" she whispered.

"That's right. In fact, some of the girls in her sew-
ing circle at church snubbed Cordia for a while because their own boyfriends were trying to call on
her. And there's another story about a young man
who threatened to climb to the top of the church
steeple and jump off when she wouldn't go riding
with him in his buggy."

"Well, it sounds as if it wasn't her fault," Melanie
said defensively. "She couldn't help it if the boys
thought she was gorgeous and totally irresistible."

Gran Pennington laughed. "Oh, she could have
helped it if she'd wanted to. The truth is, she was a
flirt! In fact, according to some, she usually had two
or three beaus at once, and she tried to keep each one
from knowing about the others. Can you imagine a
thing like that?"

Melanie gulped and looked down at the album where Great-great-grandmother Cordia smiled at her. What would Gran Pennington think if she knew how much her own granddaughter loved to flirt? And that Melanie always had two or three crushes of her own?

"Thumb on through the album, if you like," suggested Gran Pennington. "There are pictures in it of Cordia with several of her boyfriends, or beaus, as she called them. Let's see . . ." Gran reached over and flipped a few pages. "Here she is again with one of them."

Melanie felt a ripple of excitement at the sight of the happy couple, smiling at each other instead of the camera. Cordia was sitting in a swing tied to the leafy branch of a tree, and she was looking up at a blond-haired boy who seemed about to give the swing a push. Under the picture were the faded words: *John, my very best beau.* "Oh," Melanie sighed aloud, trying to imagine herself in the very same pose with Scott or Shane or Garrett.

"Take the album home with you, if you'd like," Gran Pennington offered. "I'm sure you'll enjoy looking through it, and you can bring it back when you've finished."

Melanie smiled appreciatively as her grandmother went on, "Here. Look in the trunk. She saved a whole bundle of love letters from young men who wanted to court her. She tied them in a pink ribbon, and they're in here with the other family albums and some other papers and letters that I've collected over the years."

Melanie's eyes brightened. Love letters? The idea was so romantic that it made a lump form in her throat. Maybe someday someone will write love letters to me, she thought. Maybe Scott or Shane or maybe someone I haven't even met yet.

"I'll just go down and do some things in the kitchen, and you can look through the trunk to your heart's content. You may find all sorts of information for your genealogy project. How's that?"

"Gosh. Thanks, Gran. That would be super."

As soon as her grandmother left, Melanie knelt before the old trunk and carefully lifted the lid. It was filled with yellowed papers and fragile photograph albums just as Gran had said it would be, and a stale, musty odor drifted into the air. She wanted to look at everything, but first she had to find Great-great-grandmother Cordia's love letters.

Beneath the first layer she found them. The pink ribbon was faded and the bow flattened from years in the trunk, but Cordia Mae Lee's name was on the front of every envelope.

With trembling hands she lifted the packet out of the trunk and placed it in her lap. Then she slid the first letter from under the pink ribbon and opened it.

CHAPTER

6

The old-fashioned handwriting was slanted and hard to read. *My dearest Cordia,* it began.

> *I have been watching you during church, praying that your eyes would meet mine and that you would smile at me the same way you did that Sunday last month at the church picnic.*

Melanie giggled. Gran was right. Cordia had been a flirt!

> *Your smile was so warm and sweet that I thought surely you cared for me as much as I care*

for you. But now I fear that I was mistaken. If
you really do care, please meet me by the poplar
tree behind the church next Sunday morning before
the service.

> *Your devoted admirer,*
> *Ben*

Melanie clasped the letter to her heart, trying to
picture Ben's face and deciding that he was probably
very handsome. "I wonder if she met him," she
whispered out loud. "And I wonder if he was the one
she married."

Quickly Melanie turned to the next letter in the
stack and began to read it. It was from a young man
named John. Melanie gasped. He was the one in the
picture who was ready to push her in the swing.
And Cordia had written *my very best beau* under the
picture.

My beloved Cordia,
I have been worried sick these last few days. It
seems so long a time since you favored me with a
smile. Is something wrong? Have I offended you?
I beg your humble pardon if I have. Please give
me a sign that you still care for me.

> *Yours forever,*
> *John*

"'Yours forever,'" Melanie repeated just above a

whisper. She sighed deeply and closed her eyes, seeing Cordia twirling a lock of her reddish-brown hair and smiling softly as she read this very letter from John all those years ago. If he was her very best beau, surely they had gotten back together. But what if they hadn't? She wished she could call to Cordia back through the years and urge her to smile at John again and to smile at Ben, also. *I* certainly would, she thought.

Slowly she picked up a third letter, from Charles, who was equally infatuated with Cordia and who had also thought she liked him but was having doubts when he wrote the letter. One after another, the letters sounded similar. The one from Jacob, the one from Aaron, the one from Robert, all swearing their devotion and begging her to care for them, too.

Melanie was deep in her reading when her grandmother called up from downstairs. "Dinner will be ready in fifteen minutes, dear. Would you like me to call your mother and see if it's all right for you to stay?"

"Eeek," squealed Melanie, pulling herself into the present and looking around the room. She hadn't realized that it was so late. "Sorry, Gran. I've got tons of homework so I'll have to go home. I'll be down in a couple of minutes."

Melanie looked at the pile of letters in her lap. She wanted to go on reading them. There was something almost magic in holding them in her hands and knowing that they had been sent to someone very much like herself so long ago. She could almost see Cordia's flirtatious smile as she bestowed it on first one young man and then another, and feel her great-great-grandmother's heart skip a beat when the smile was returned. "I know just how she felt," Melanie murmured, reluctantly putting the letter she held back on top of the packet. I absolutely have to come back and read more of them tomorrow.

She retied the letters with the pink bow and started to put them back into the trunk when she noticed another letter. It was addressed to Gran Pennington, and her own mother's return address was in the corner. What caught her eye was the postmark, only seven months before her own birth, and Gran's notation on the envelope: *News that Kathy's going to have a baby.*

Melanie stared at the letter for a moment. Kathy was her mother's name, and her family had lived in another city from the time her parents were married until they moved to their present home when Melanie entered second grade at Mark Twain Elementary. It gave her a tingly feeling to see the letter lying there and know that it was about her before she was even born.

Should I read it, or shouldn't I? she wondered. Shaking her head, she placed Cordia's love letters back in the trunk and started to close the lid. Still, she reasoned, Gran said to look through the trunk as much as I wanted to. She didn't say there were things I shouldn't see.

Slowly Melanie lifted the trunk lid again. She could see the corner of her grandmother's letter peeking out from under the stack of letters tied with the pink ribbon. Using two fingers like pincers, she slowly pulled the letter out and held it up, reading the notation on the front one more time. *News that Kathy's going to have a baby.*

"It's about *me*," Melanie said aloud. "So I'm going to read it."

She felt a glow of anticipation as she pulled the pages out of the envelope. It was going to be exciting to read about how she was going to be born. *Dear Mom*, the letter began.

> *I know you've been wondering why I haven't written in such a long time and that you always say that no news is good news, but the truth is, I haven't been sure if the news I'm going to tell you is good news or not.*

Melanie gasped softly. What had her mother meant? This certainly wasn't what she had expected to read. The letter went on:

> *Larry and I had planned to wait awhile to have*

a baby. You know how I've worked for years to become a concert pianist and have given up a lot to achieve my dream. But accidents happen, I guess, and now I'll have to forget that dream.

The words blurred before Melanie's eyes as their meaning slowly sunk in. "An *accident!*" she whispered. "They didn't plan for me to be born. They didn't even *want* me!"

With trembling fingers, she folded the letter and put it back into the envelope, stuffing it under an old photograph album. She didn't want to read the second page. She already knew what the letter said, *and it was awful.*

Melanie sat in the growing shadows of the old-fashioned bedroom, staring at the crumbling photo album in the trunk and thinking about the letter underneath it. Her mother had said she wanted to be a concert pianist, but now she couldn't. She couldn't because she was going to have a baby. "And that baby turned out to be me," Melanie whispered.

It took all the acting skill that she possessed to go downstairs and face her grandmother without letting the emotions she was feeling show. She kissed Gran Pennington on the cheek as she clutched the album containing Cordia's pictures and headed for home.

When she reached her own house a few minutes later, she hesitated an instant before going inside.

How was she going to face her parents knowing what she knew now? All these years they had pretended to love her when all the time they were only faking. How could they love her? she reasoned, when she had spoiled her mother's chances for a wonderful career. Without me, she would probably be famous right now, thought Melanie, and rich!

Melanie tiptoed through the kitchen, hoping her mother would not look up from the pot she was stirring on the stove, but of course she did.

"Hi, honey," she said brightly. "Did you get all the information you need from your gran?"

A lump jumped into Melanie's throat, and when she tried to say yes, only a squeak came out, so she nodded and hurried to her room. She was in a fog all through dinner, and later she couldn't remember what she had eaten. She stayed in her room until bedtime pretending to work on homework, but instead the words of the letter burned in her mind. *You know how I've worked for years to become a concert pianist and have given up a lot to achieve my dream. But accidents happen* . . .

Melanie thought about the piano downstairs in the living room. She knew her mother played extremely well. Sometimes she even played for weddings or special programs at church. But why hadn't she ever mentioned to Melanie that she had wanted to be a concert pianist? Why? she asked over and over again. Then she shuddered. Maybe it was because she wanted to be a concert pianist so much that it hurt to talk about it.

Next her thoughts turned to her own attempts at piano lessons when she was in third grade. It had been fun for a while, but then she got tired of practicing and gave it up. Melanie sighed sadly at the memory. Just one more way I've disappointed her, she thought.

Her mind was still on her mother when she got to school the next morning, and she was so absorbed in her own thoughts that she didn't hear Funny come running up to her.

"Melanie! Guess what?" Funny chirped. "I talked to my parents last night just the way you said I should, and do you know what they told me?"

Melanie pulled herself out of the fog she was in and looked at her smiling friend.

"No," she said, shaking her head. "What did they say?"

"They said I really am a Hawthorne because all the traditions and attitudes that have been passed down through the generations have shaped our family and helped make me the kind of person I am. That's kind of complicated, but I think I understand. It means that the things they've taught me ever since I was a baby came partly from our ancestors."

Funny paused to catch her breath, and Melanie tried to answer, but the words stuck in her throat.

"And that's not all," gushed Funny. "They said I'm extraspecial because I'm adopted. They wanted a baby so badly and then they picked *me* out, and that makes me a *chosen* child. Isn't that super? And all the time I thought I was a nobody."

Melanie gulped hard, stunned by these last words, and stared at Funny as tears rolled down her cheeks.

CHAPTER

7

*M*elanie raced for the girls' bathroom as the bell rang for morning classes to begin. She couldn't face her friends or her teachers or anyone right now. Not until she had sorted things out.

The bathroom was empty and she hurried to a sink and splashed cold water onto her face. Her nose was red and her eyes watery, and she fished around in her purse for a tissue.

How could things have turned around so completely? she wondered as she blew her nose loudly. Yesterday she had felt so secure and loved by her own family and had been trying to convince Funny Hawthorne not to think of herself as a nobody because she was adopted. But today everything was different. Everything was *wrong*. It was Funny who felt secure and loved because her parents had said she was *wanted* and *chosen*.

"But I'm just an accident," she whispered to herself in the mirror. "Nobody wanted me. I just wrecked everything for my parents."

Melanie slumped against the wall beside the sink and looked at the door. The school was quiet. Classes had started. She would have to stay in the girls' bathroom until her face was no longer red and then go to the office for a tardy slip. What excuse could she give?

"I've been in the bathroom crying because my parents didn't really want me," she mumbled. "Sure. I can hear it all now," she added sarcastically.

Melanie thought back over the past few days. Her mother had yelled at her for putting her books on the kitchen table and forgetting to take them up to her room. She was always yelling at Melanie for things like that, but Jeffy got away with everything. And there was the business about keeping her room picked up. Her mother was an absolute broken record about that. But did she ever fuss at Jeffy to pick up his room? Of course not. She did it herself. If that wasn't proof that her mother didn't love her, what was? And what about all those times when she was younger when she had real, honest-to-goodness, *genuine* stomachaches, but her mother hadn't believed her and made her go to school anyway? Then there was the pet situation. Melanie had begged and pleaded most of her life for a pet, but what had her parents always said? No. It wasn't until they saw Rainbow at the animal shelter and fell in love with the little dog themselves that they gave in. Now that she thought about it, there were at least a million times that her parents had rejected her, but she had been too blind to see it then.

Melanie chewed her lower lip and thought the situation over. What she really wanted to do was go home. Her mother would be there, taking care of Jeffy before she drove him to his afternoon kindergarten class. Maybe if she watched her mother closely, she would find more proof that she was really just a burden to the family. She had to admit that it was different with Jeffy. Her mother's career had already been wrecked by the time he came along. They had adjusted. Made the best of a bad situation. They were ready for him. But still, it didn't make her feel any better. And it didn't make her want to stay at school and face everyone either.

"But what if I pretend I'm sick?" she whispered. She liked that idea. All she would have to do was convince the school nurse. So what if her mother never believed her? She would have to believe a real nurse. Glancing into the mirror, she pinched her nose to bring the redness back and then slipped into the hall.

The nurse's office was just around the corner, and Melanie was glad to see that no other students were there. She would never be able to lie to the nurse if she had an audience, especially if that audience was anyone she knew.

The nurse, Miss Byars, looked up from her paperwork when Melanie walked in. "Good morning. What can I do for you?"

Melanie took a deep breath. "I'm not feeling well," she said in a small voice. "My stomach hurts, and I think I might throw up."

"Oh, dear," said Miss Byars. She tucked a strand of dark hair behind her ear and looked at Melanie with solemn brown eyes. "You do look a little flushed. Perhaps you'd better sit down."

Melanie nodded and sank into the chair beside the desk. It felt awful to lie, but right now it seemed like the only thing to do. Besides, Miss Byars hadn't given her the third degree to see if she was lying about the stomachache. Miss Byars had believed her, not like *some* people she could name.

"Is someone at home who can come for you?" Miss Byars asked. "I'd be glad to call for you."

"My mom's there," Melanie said flatly. She gave the nurse her phone number and watched out of the corner of her eye as Miss Byars punched in the numbers. Several seconds passed but nothing happened.

"It's ringing," Miss Byars said cheerfully.

More seconds passed but still nothing happened. Melanie frowned. Where is she? Why doesn't she answer the phone?

"Maybe I rang the wrong number," the nurse offered. "I'll try again."

But nobody answered this time either. "She's probably gone out for a few minutes," said Melanie.

"Would you like to lie down for now, and then I could try again later?" asked the nurse.

Melanie looked at the small metal cot jutting out from the wall. It was in plain view of anyone who might happen to come into the nurse's office. She would die if she had to lie down there and *double* die if anyone she knew came in and saw her. "No," she said hurriedly. "I'd just like to go home."

Miss Byars nodded and then opened a small file box sitting on her desk, thumbed through, and pulled out a card.

"It says here to contact Mrs. Clare Miller if your mother isn't home."

"That's our next-door neighbor," said Melanie.

"Then I'll be glad to phone her for you," said the nurse. "Are you sure you wouldn't like to lie down?"

Melanie shook her head and watched apprehensively as Miss Byars keyed in Mrs. Miller's number.

What if her mother was out for the day, shopping or something? What good would it do to go home if there was no one there to spy on? Maybe she should say that she was feeling better and go back to class. But what was really bothering her was why her mother hadn't answered the phone. It doesn't matter that I'm sick and need to come home, she thought. She and Jeffy are probably out somewhere having a great time. They probably went ice skating at the rink at the mall. Or maybe Mom took Jeffy to story hour at the library.

"Hello, Mrs. Miller?" she heard Miss Byars say. "This is the school nurse at Wakeman Junior High. I'm calling for Melanie Edwards. She isn't feeling well, but her mother doesn't answer the phone. Oh, she is? That's wonderful. May I speak with her, please?"

Melanie jumped to attention as Miss Byars gave her a reassuring smile and waited for Mrs. Edwards to come to the phone. So what if she was only at Mrs. Miller's, Melanie thought grumpily. She still wasn't home when I needed her.

Her mother was at school within fifteen minutes, and even Melanie had to admit that she looked worried. "What's wrong, honey?"

"My stomach's a little upset. That's all," she murmured.

"Well, let's take you home," she said, putting an

arm around Melanie. Turning to Miss Byars, she said, "I'm sorry I wasn't home when you called. Jeffy and I ran next door to borrow an egg from Mrs. Miller. We stayed longer than we meant to because she wanted to show us how she's taught her little dog, Jo-Jo, to roll over and shake hands."

"Of course, Mrs. Edwards," Miss Byars reassured her. "You couldn't have known that Melanie was going to get sick this morning."

Mrs. Edwards thanked the nurse again and led Melanie out to the car where Jeffy was waiting. As she trudged toward the car, Melanie realized that she did actually feel a little sick. There was a dull ache in her head and her stomach was starting to gurgle. Maybe I wasn't lying after all, she told herself.

The smell of brownies hit Melanie as soon as she stepped in the front door of her house. She drifted into the kitchen and put her books down on the kitchen counter. There were the brownies, her mother's specialty, on a platter. Nearby the other bowls and utensils sat where her mother had left them when she went next door to borrow an egg.

"I wish you'd told me you weren't feeling well before you went out in the cold this morning," said Mrs. Edwards, coming up behind Melanie and feeling her forehead with the back of her hand. "You don't seem to have any fever, but maybe you'd better scoot on up to your room and jump into bed. The rest will do you good. Jeffy and I'll try to be extra quiet in case you want to sleep, won't we, Jeffy?"

Jeffy nodded and jumped up to his usual place at the counter, grabbing a mixing bowl and cleaning it with his finger, and her mother gave Melanie a sympathetic smile before walking over and tousling his hair.

Tears filled Melanie's eyes as she watched the two of them. They seemed so happy, so natural together, and she felt suddenly apart from them. It was as if a cold, invisible curtain had been pulled in between them and her. She wiped the back of her hand across her eyes, turned on her heel, and left the room.

CHAPTER

8

*M*elanie dropped her books on her desk and sat down. Now what was she going to do? Her mother had sent her to her room. Melanie bristled. That way, I won't be able to see what's really going on around here.

She had just changed into her nightgown when she heard her mother's footsteps coming up the stairs and then a soft knock on her door. Dashing to her bed, she ducked under the covers just as her mother said, "Honey, may I come in?"

"Okay," answered Melanie in a weak voice.

Mrs. Edwards came into the room and sat down on the edge of Melanie's bed. "Is there anything I can get for you before Jeffy and I run to the grocery store? Is your stomach still upset? Would you like some Alka-Seltzer?"

Melanie stared at her mother in astonishment. Here I am sick, she thought, and she's running off to the grocery store.

When Melanie didn't answer, her mother reached out and touched her forehead again. "Still no fever," she said hopefully. "I think you've just let yourself get too tired. A day's rest will do you good. Now you just snuggle down into the covers and try to sleep while Jeffy and I are gone."

She glared at the door after her mother left. Any other mother would have stayed home with a sick child, she grumped to herself. But not my mother. She can't stand to be in the same house with me. So what if I'm sick? I could *die* and she probably wouldn't care.

Things were crazy. Only yesterday she had been super happy, thinking she had everything and feeling sorry for Funny Hawthorne. But Funny had one thing that she didn't have, and it meant more than anything else. Funny's parents wanted her.

When she heard her mother's car pull out of the driveway, she got up and hurried to the basement. There was someone there she could talk to, she thought, someone who would listen.

When she flipped on the light, Rainbow blinked

up at her from the box where she was snuggled with her eight puppies. Seeing Melanie, she raised her head and gave Melanie a smile.

She knelt beside the box stroking first Rainbow and then each of the fat, squirming puppies, remembering how she and her friends had rescued Rainbow and fourteen other dogs and cats from being put to sleep at the animal shelter on Christmas Eve. Rainbow had been Melanie's favorite because of her gentle eyes and her multicolored coat, which was why she had been given her name.

"Nobody wanted you either, did they, Rainbow?" she whispered.

Rainbow laid her head in Melanie's hand and whimpered softly.

"But *I* did. And I always will."

Melanie hurried back to her room and lay in bed wrapped in gloom the rest of the morning, pretending to be asleep when her mother knocked softly on the door and called that she was home from shopping. She even kept quiet at lunchtime, hoping her growling stomach wouldn't make so much noise that it would give her away. But each time her mother came to the door and then tiptoed away again, Melanie felt tears welling up. Why didn't she just come on in? Melanie wondered. Why doesn't she check on me or insist I eat lunch? Maybe she just doesn't want to be around me.

But by afternoon Melanie was feeling restless, and she slipped out of bed and got Cordia's photograph album off her desk. "I wonder what Cordia did when she was feeling ill?" Melanie whispered, glancing around the room and giggling softly. Then she put the album on her bedside table, plumped her pillows, and climbed back into bed, reclining elegantly, the way she imagined Cordia would, and opening the album in her lap.

She turned again to the picture of her great-great-grandmother, sitting in the swing with John standing behind her. "John certainly *is* handsome," she murmured. She looked closer. There seemed to be something almost familiar about him. Did his blond hair make him look a little like Scott Daly, or was it wishful thinking? The idea gave her an eerie feeling, and she got up and looked into her mirror. *She* looked like Cordia, and now *Scott* looked like one of Cordia's beaus. *My best beau*, Cordia had written under the picture. And wasn't Scott her best beau, too?

Melanie piled her shoulder-length hair onto her head, turning to first one side and then the other as she tried to imagine being Cordia Mae Lee almost one hundred years ago. Sucking in her breath, she whispered, "I *do* look like her. Oh, I wish I could have been her. She was so lucky. Everybody loved her, especially all those gorgeous boys. I wonder

what it would be like to have boys writing me letters, *begging* me to like them or threatening to throw
themselves off church steeples if I didn't go riding
with them?" She frowned, thinking of Scott and
Shane and Garrett and how all three of them were
ignoring her. Oh, if only I could be more like Cordia, she thought.

She plopped onto the bed again and turned to
another page in the album only to find Great-great-
grandmother Cordia building a snowman with
another young man. Her cheeks were glowing as she
held her long skirt up out of the snow with one hand
and patted the snowman's chest with the other. Her
"beau" was standing back, looking at Cordia and the
snowman as if he were deciding which one he liked
best.

He's a cool one, thought Melanie. Cool and full of
self-confidence, like Shane. The thought startled
her so much that she gasped out loud. Underneath
the picture Cordia had written: *Charles, my mysterious
beau.* Shane wasn't exactly mysterious, but at least
he was different.

Melanie lay back against her pillows and stared at
the ceiling, marveling at how much she and Cordia
were alike. Even their boyfriends had a lot in common. "And just think," she whispered, "if it hadn't
been for Mrs. Clark's genealogy project, I would
never have known."

Later in the day Jeffy yelled that supper was ready. Melanie got up and brushed her hair. She was just too hungry to stay in her room any longer. Besides, thinking about her genealogy project again had reminded her of her parents, and that had brought back her black mood. She had to find out if anyone even *cared* that she was sick.

When she joined the others at the table, Jeffy was telling his parents, in great detail, about a movie he had seen on television that afternoon after school. She stood beside her chair, waiting to see if anyone would notice her.

"And then Godzilla went crashing through the jungle looking for his baby, Godzooki, who was hiding in a cave," Jeffy was saying. Mrs. Edwards was smiling in the right places as he told the story, and Melanie's father looked up from his plate periodically to show he was listening.

Melanie couldn't stop the little feeling of resentment that was creeping into her stomach. She cleared her throat.

"Hello, sweetheart," her mother said. "I'm glad you're feeling well enough to eat some supper. I wasn't thinking when I fixed spaghetti. I hope it isn't too spicy for your stomach."

"Sorry to hear that you're not feeling well," said her father, but before she could answer, Jeffy was talking about his movie again.

Melanie sighed and picked at her spaghetti, waiting for her turn at conversation again. "I told you that I went to Gran Pennington's yesterday," she said when Jeffy finally paused to take a breath. She looked directly at each of her parents when she spoke, but except for a quick glance from her mother, neither of them showed any outward signs of interest in what she had said.

Melanie lifted her voice and tried to sound more perky. "But I forgot to mention that she showed me *all* her old picture albums. Boy, did we have some weird-looking ancestors."

Jeffy spun a big wad of spaghetti on his fork and tried to jam it, stringers and all, into his mouth.

"Jeffrey!" her mother scolded him. "Don't eat like a little pig!"

"There were several pictures of Great-great-grandma Cordia Mae Lee," Melanie continued, trying to find a way to attract their attention to what she was saying. "She was really pretty, and Gran thinks I look like her."

Mr. Edwards ignored Melanie and pointed a finger commandingly at Jeffy. "Listen to your mother and eat correctly."

Melanie sank down in her chair and stabbed at her spaghetti and pulled up a large forkful.

"Melanie!" her mother said in a shocked voice. "What are you doing?"

"Can't we have any peace at the dinner table?" her father asked angrily. He shoved his chair back, got up, and left the room, leaving the others to stare after him.

Melanie's chin quivered, and the weight of the fork and spaghetti felt like a thousand tons. She had only been trying to make conversation, and they wouldn't pay any attention to her. She hadn't done anything wrong. A huge lump grew in her throat so she couldn't swallow.

"May I be excused?" she asked in a tiny voice.

Her mother's face looked as if she had suddenly gotten very tired as she gave her consent with a limp wave of her hand.

Back in her room, Melanie flopped across her bed. She had been right. Nobody in her family really cared about her. Jeffy got all the attention by talking about dumb movies he had seen on TV and acting like a cute little boy. The thought hurt her. Jeffy *was* a cute little boy, and she loved him, and she shouldn't take it out on him just because her parents hadn't wanted her.

She sighed. It was awful knowing that her parents hadn't wanted her and that she really was a nobody right here in her own home. I wonder what it's like in Funny's family? she thought. They probably listen to everything she has to say. It's no wonder her family gave her the nickname Funny. She's probably the happiest person on earth. And I'll bet that they give her everything she wants and ask her opinion when they're making important decisions.

The more Melanie thought about the Hawthorne family, the more curious she became, until a very interesting idea began forming in her mind.

CHAPTER

*A*t the fence on the school ground the next morn-ing, Jana, Katie, Christie, and Beth crowded around Melanie, all asking questions at once.

"What happened to you yesterday?" asked Christie.

"Yeah," said Katie. "I saw you before class yester-day morning, and then you disappeared."

"I called your house after school, but your mom said you couldn't come to the phone because you were sick," said Jana.

Melanie debated whether or not to tell them the truth, but after all, she decided, they were her best friends.

"I was faking being sick," she announced. "I

found out something awful about myself while I was working on the genealogy project, and I decided to go back home and spy on my mom to see if it was true."

Beth gasped. "What did you find out?"

Melanie took a deep breath. It was hard to admit the truth, even to her best friends. "My parents didn't want me to be born," she stated flatly. "My mom had planned a big career as a concert pianist, and I wrecked it."

"Oh, come on, Mel," Katie said seriously. "You know your parents wanted you."

"No, they didn't. I read a letter Mom wrote to my grandmother, and in it she said"—Melanie paused dramatically—"I was an *accident*." She went on to tell them more about the letter and how she had found it in the trunk at her grandmother's house.

Christie frowned. "So, what did playing sick yesterday prove?"

"Everything I had started suspecting," insisted Melanie. "The only time my mom ever pays any attention to me is when she's yelling at me. Can you believe that she didn't even stay around the house to take care of me when I came home sick? She and Jeffy left practically as soon as I got there."

"Gosh, Melanie," said Jana. "I don't think that means she doesn't love you. You said yourself that you were faking being sick. Maybe she could tell. You know how mothers are."

"She couldn't tell," grumped Melanie. "Besides, by that time I really was feeling sick. And that's not all. Both my parents really ate it up when Jeffy told the plot of an entire *long* television movie at the dinner table last night, but did they pay attention to me when I had something to say? Of course not. My mom just yelled again about my table manners."

"Hey, my mom yells at me all the time, too," teased Beth. "And to think that until now I believed she really loved me."

"I think you're wrong, too," said Katie. "Look at how she doesn't want to work outside the home so that she can be there for you and Jeffy. And don't forget about those scrumptious brownies that she's always *forcing* us to eat when we're at your house."

"She bakes those for Jeffy," Melanie said angrily.

"Jeffy's not a member of The Fabulous Five," Jana reminded her with a grin.

Melanie shrugged. Her friends just didn't understand. So what if her mother baked brownies? Big deal! That didn't prove she'd really wanted Melanie. Glancing away, Melanie promised herself that she would spend most of the weekend spying and getting evidence that even The Fabulous Five wouldn't be able to argue with.

Nobody said anything for a few minutes, and Melanie knew that it was her fault. Her bad mood had affected her friends, too, but she couldn't help it. They just didn't realize how awful it was to be unwanted. Probably Scott didn't want her for a girlfriend anymore, either, she thought. Maybe he was tired of her or he had found someone else. Shane was too busy worrying about Igor to care about her now. Imagine! she scoffed silently, an iguana's love life being more important than his own. And Garrett. Well, she mused, after all, he is in eighth grade. How interested could he get in a seventh-grader like me?

Melanie was still moping around when she got to her locker a little while later. She was trying for the third time to open her stubborn combination lock when Funny came racing up to her.

"Hi," Funny said, grinning broadly. "Where were you yesterday? I looked all over for you at lunchtime, but everyone said you were absent."

Melanie breathed a sigh and tried to return Funny's smile, but she couldn't.

"Oh, I wasn't feeling very well so I went home," she lied.

"Well, I'm glad you're back today," said Funny. "Especially since today is our Family Living field trip to do gravestone rubbings at the cemetery. I've got to run. See you later."

Melanie watched Funny speed down the hall, thinking about the field trip. She had forgotten all about it, but maybe it would be the perfect time to talk to Funny about her idea.

Family Living students from both Mrs. Clark's and Mrs. Blankenship's classes pushed and jammed onto two school buses for the trip to the cemetery that afternoon. Melanie could see Funny ahead of her in the crowd, but by the time she jostled her way onto the bus, Jana and Funny were sitting together. Melanie squeezed into the seat behind them next to Kim Baxter. Neither Funny nor Jana had even so much as said hello to her. Some friends, she thought. Just because I'm in a bad mood doesn't mean that I'm poison.

Jana was by the window and Funny on the aisle, and across the aisle from Funny was Shane. He hadn't said anything to Melanie either. When the bus started moving, she closed her eyes, trying to fight down the misery that was overtaking her. Suddenly she heard Shane shout above the noisy crowd.

"Hey, Funny," he called. "You and Jana wouldn't happen to know any female iguanas, would you?"

Melanie perked up and listened in spite of herself.

"Sure. There's Mrs. Clark and Mrs. Blankenship and Miss Dickinson and . . . let's see. Who else?" teased Funny. Beside her Jana was laughing like crazy.

When Melanie realized that she was chuckling, too, she looked quickly away. She didn't want anyone to make her laugh. She had a perfect right to feel miserable.

She tried not to listen, but she heard Shane say, "Naw. They're not Igor's type. You don't know what a problem it is to find him a girlfriend. He's so particular."

"Yeah, I know the feeling," said Jana, and Melanie could tell from the tone of her voice that she was only pretending to be sympathetic.

"Yesterday my dad got this great idea to take him to the zoo," Shane went on. "It sounded like a pretty good idea to me. There must be dozens of iguanas out there, and surely even someone as choosy as Igor could find a girlfriend in that crowd."

Funny leaned into the aisle. "So, what happened?" she pressed.

"Absolutely nothing. The reptile keeper agreed to let him into the pen, and Igor walked around for a while and then wanted to go home. He said all the babes were stuck up and spoiled because of easy living at the zoo. Can you believe that? So now we're back to square one."

All around, kids were laughing at Shane's story, and Melanie sank back in her seat. Listening to him talk about Igor's love problems would ordinarily have made her feel better, but not this time. Not when she was feeling terminally depressed.

"Okay, everybody," said Mrs. Clark when the buses unloaded just inside the gates of the cemetery a few minutes later and the students from her classes gathered around her. "I have all the supplies right here to begin making our rubbings, but first, I want everyone to pick a gravestone. If it belongs to someone from your own family, you may use the gold crayons to show that your rubbing is special."

"But isn't it bad luck to step on a grave?" asked Marcie Bee.

Richie Corrierro crept forward in a monster pose, his eyes wide and his hands raised like claws as if he were about to grab someone. "Of course it is, my dear," he said in a sinister voice. "The ghosts of the people buried there will rise up and GET YOU!"

Marcie shrieked as he jumped toward her, and small screams rippled through the crowd. Melanie shuddered. She didn't believe in ghosts, but still . . . they were nothing to joke about.

"That's enough, Richie," Mrs. Clark said, glaring at him. "That's just an old superstition," she went on, smiling kindly at Marcie. "As long as we are all *well mannered and behave ourselves*"—she paused, looking at Richie again—"we have nothing to worry about. Now run along, boys and girls, and find your

stones so that we can get started making our rubbings."

Melanie was standing a little way apart from the
others, and she shaded her eyes with a hand and
glanced out over the field of tombstones in the direction Gran Pennington had said she would find Cordia Mae Lee's grave. All of the stones were old, and
some went back as far as the Revolutionary War, but
many were even older, dating to the first settlers.
They were mostly small stones with scrolly writing
and curved tops. Some had pictures of angels carved
on them or of sailing ships or open books that were
probably meant to represent the Bible.

After she got her bearings, Melanie went straight
toward her great-great-grandmother's grave as boys
and girls scattered through the rows like an army of
bugs. She could see Jana three rows over, marching
in the same direction, but she didn't even look
Melanie's way. Behind her, she could hear Mrs.
Clark scolding Clarence Marshall for broad-jumping
over the gravestones, but most kids, she noticed,
were being careful to walk around the graves.

Finally she knelt in front of the tiny white stone
bearing her great-great-grandmother's name.

Cordia Mae Lee Gardner
Born October 4, 1896
Died March 7, 1955

Gardner would have been her married name, Melanie thought, wondering if he had been one of the young men who had written Cordia letters, or better still, if he had been in one of the pictures in her great-great-grandmother's album. Perhaps he was John, the one Cordia had called her best beau, or Charles, her mysterious beau.

Reaching forward, she rubbed a finger over the words on the stone, feeling a sense of relief. At least here was someone who would understand her. If only Cordia were here to talk to her now.

CHAPTER

10

*J*ust then Mrs. Clark came bustling up. "What color crayon would you like?" she asked, handing Melanie the other supplies she needed for her rubbing.

"Gold," Melanie said proudly. "This is my great-great-grandmother's tombstone."

Mrs. Clark nodded appreciatively. "Have you learned a lot of interesting things about her from your family that you can share with the class?"

Melanie swallowed a giggle. "Yes . . . um . . . I think so."

The teacher gave her a gold crayon, nodded again, and moved on.

Melanie busied herself taping the heavy paper

over the lettering, wishing again that she could talk to Cordia.

"If you were here," she said softly, "I'd tell you about my boyfriends and ask you how to get them to pay more attention to me." Melanie sighed. "Shane didn't even look at me when he was telling the story about Igor on the bus," she went on. "I don't think he likes me anymore."

She picked up the gold crayon and gently rubbed it against the surface, watching the letters and numbers magically appear on the paper. "And Scott acts as if I'm invisible. I'll bet you'd know what to do. You were a real expert on things like that."

Suddenly she pushed too hard and her crayon zipped right off the edge of the stone, landing in the grass. When she reached for it, she noticed for the first time that Scott was working on a rubbing only two stones away. Had he chosen that tombstone on purpose so that he could be near her?

Melanie giggled as she reached for the crayon. It was almost as if she had received a message from Great-great-grandmother Cordia to look in that direction. Otherwise she might not have noticed him for ages.

The idea gave her a creepy feeling and she started to work on her rubbing again when another thought occurred to her. Maybe Cordia was answering her questions about her boyfriends. Maybe she was saying that Melanie should flirt with Scott even though he had been ignoring her. Maybe she was even saying that she should concentrate on Scott and forget about Shane—at least for now. Of course, she thought gleefully. That has to be it! The rotten mood she had been in earlier suddenly disappeared.

Melanie smoothed her long hair with one hand. Then she took a deep breath and called as sweetly as she could, "Hi, Scott, what color crayon are you using?"

"Green," he replied matter-of-factly, but Melanie was certain she could detect a tiny smile playing around the corners of his mouth. She had been right. She was supposed to flirt with him, after all.

"Mine's gold because this is where my great-great-grandmother is buried," she bragged. "Come here a minute and I'll show you how gorgeous this rubbing is going to be when I'm finished."

Scott got to his feet slowly, but Melanie couldn't help noticing that he reached her in an instant and knelt beside her in the grass. Then he took a long look at the rubbing as if it were the most interesting thing he had seen in a long time.

"Yeah, that's really nice," he said, darting quick looks at her out of the corner of his eyes.

Melanie had to fight down an urge to giggle with delight. What would I ever have done without Great-great-grandmother Cordia? she wondered.

She scooted a little bit closer to him and said

softly, "Her life was *sooooo* romantic. I know because I read all of her love letters. They're tied together with a pink ribbon, and my grandmother keeps them in an old trunk."

"Wow," said Scott, looking at her in astonishment. "But didn't you feel funny reading them? I mean . . . aren't they kind of personal?"

Melanie's mind raced to find an answer. She didn't want him to think she was a snoop. "Don't forget what Mrs. Clark said about learning things from studying our ancestors," she said quickly. Then she added coyly, "I'm learning a lot of things about love from reading her letters."

Scott fidgeted slightly, then raised his eyes to meet hers. "You are?" he asked shyly, but Melanie was sure she detected a hopeful sound in his voice.

She nodded, glancing gratefully at Cordia's gravestone and then back at Scott again. Next, she would simply ask to see his gravestone rubbing and compliment him on how beautiful it was. Then she would ask him about his ancestors, and by then he would probably have forgotten all about whatever it was that had made him ignore her lately. In fact, he might even be ready to ask her out again.

Suddenly Mrs. Clark spoiled everything by peeking around a tall monument with a winged angel on top and shouting, "Scott Daly. Are you finished with your rubbing?"

Scott jumped to his feet. "Not yet," he said in a flustered voice.

"We're leaving in twenty minutes, so you'd better get busy."

Scott nodded to Mrs. Clark and bounded toward his own gravestone, stopping halfway there to look back at Melanie.

"I've got to get busy," he said, echoing Mrs. Clark.

"Sure," said Melanie demurely. "I understand. I'll talk to you later."

Scott nodded again and set to work on his rubbing. Melanie knelt in front of her great-great-grandmother's gravestone again and picked up the gold crayon. Glancing around quickly to make sure no one was near enough to notice, she leaned toward the stone and whispered, "Thanks. That really worked. I think he likes me again."

She waited for a moment, although she didn't really expect an answer from Cordia, and then she began working on the rubbing again, humming to herself as she worked. It took only a few more moments to finish the rubbing, and she rocked back onto her heels and looked at it with pleasure.

"It's beautiful," she said out loud. But then she noticed one spot on the upper right-hand side where she had missed. She leaned forward and poised the gold crayon in front of her when something caught her eye just above the tombstone. She squinted and looked again over the spot she had forgotten to color on the rubbing. She sucked in her breath. She was looking straight at Shane!

Melanie gulped. Was she getting another message from Great-great-grandmother Cordia?

"Of course I am," she whispered, and then she thought, otherwise why would I have forgotten to color in that teensy, tiny little bit of the gravestone rubbing? Cordia didn't want me just to notice Scott. She wanted me to notice Shane, too!

She chewed her lower lip and tried to decide what to do. But before she could come up with anything clever, Mrs. Clark and Mrs. Blankenship were both marching around the tombstones shouting for everyone to pick up their things and get ready to leave.

"The buses will be here in five minutes," called Mrs. Clark. "Untape your rubbings carefully. If you need to do more work to them, we can finish them in class Monday."

Melanie glanced back over her shoulder at Cordia's gravestone as she tucked her rubbing under her arm and headed for the buses. So what if she hadn't gotten to talk to Shane here? She would find another chance to get his attention. After all, she thought with a smile, she was positive that was exactly what her great-great-grandmother would have done.

CHAPTER

11

*O*n the bus ride back to school, Melanie thought back over the afternoon at the cemetery. She knew down deep that she hadn't really gotten any messages from her great-great-grandmother, who had been dead all these years. But still, if it hadn't been for Cordia, she might never have gotten up the courage to flirt with Scott and Shane again. Well, probably not *never*, she corrected herself. She only wished that she could have gotten the chance to talk to Shane before now.

The only other thing that had kept the afternoon from being perfect was the fact that she hadn't had the opportunity to talk to Funny and set her new plan in motion. As they were getting off the bus, she grabbed Funny's arm and asked, "Are you going to Bumpers after school?"

"Sure," Funny replied happily. "It's Friday. You know, TGIF. You're going, too, aren't you?"

Melanie nodded. "Look for me when you get there. I need to talk to you."

Funny said she would and headed for her locker since it was time for the bell dismissing classes for the day. Melanie watched her go, hoping she could pull things off the way she had planned.

When she and the rest of The Fabulous Five got to Bumpers, they had to squeeze their way through the crowd of wall-to-wall kids.

"How are we ever going to find a table?" wailed Beth over music blaring from the jukebox. "This place is a zoo."

"I know," said Katie. "I've had my foot stepped on three times already, and we're barely in the door."

"Yeah, but look at all the cute boys who are here," Melanie reminded them. She was bouncing on her toes, trying to look every direction at once. "I see Shane and Randy over there, and Tony is talking to Scott by the order counter. And isn't that Keith in the yellow bumper car?"

The girls pressed their way through the crowd, stopping every few steps to talk to friends. Finally a group of eighth-graders vacated a table near the door, and Melanie and her friends dove for it before anyone else could claim it.

"Hey, is there room for us?" shouted Shane. He was waving in their direction, but Melanie could see that he was looking straight at her.

"Sure!" she shouted back, not caring that there weren't enough chairs to go around. She would gladly give up hers if it meant that Shane was paying attention to her again. Maybe she would even sit on his lap.

Shane and Randy made their way through the crowd, holding sodas and fries high above their heads. When they reached the table, Shane plunked his food down beside Melanie and said, grinning, "Help yourself to this stuff. I'll go get something else for myself."

When he and Randy went back to the order counter, Melanie grabbed a french fry and breathed a huge sigh. "I can't believe it!" she screeched. "It's been ages since he's so much as looked in my direction. I had even decided that he didn't like me anymore." Then, thinking of her great-great-grandmother Cordia, she added, "It must be fate!" and giggled.

"Don't be silly," said Katie. "Guys get interested in boy-type things, and they need breathing room sometimes, just the way girls do."

Melanie gave her a puzzled look. "Who needs breathing room?"

Katie rolled her eyes to the ceiling and started to answer when Funny called from across the room.

"Hi, Melanie. What did you want to talk to me about?"

Melanie scrambled to her feet. "Shane can sit in my chair, and tell him I'll be right back," she instructed her friends. Then she hurried to Funny, who was trying to squeeze her way through one of the aisles.

"Let's go to the girls' bathroom," said Melanie. "It's more private."

When the door closed behind them, Melanie crossed her fingers behind her back. She hated to lie to anyone, but this was important. Taking a deep breath, she said, "I feel a little strange asking, but I was wondering if I could spend the night at your house tonight. My parents are going to be away overnight, and all of my other friends are busy. I know it's a lot to ask, and if you think The Fantastic Foursome would get mad, just say so, and I'll understand."

"Don't be silly," said Funny. "Of course they won't get mad. Besides," she said, raising an eyebrow, "who's going to tell them?"

Both girls laughed at the thought of The Fabulous Five's archrivals, The Fantastic Foursome, not knowing that the two of them were spending the night together.

"Well, do you think your parents would mind?" Melanie pressed.

"I don't know why they would," said Funny. "Of course, I'll have to ask them before I can be sure, but it sounds like fun to me. Is it okay if I talk to them as soon as I get home and then call you?"

"Great," said Melanie. "You may have just saved my life. Otherwise I'd have to go with my parents and Jeffy, and that would be totally boring."

Melanie uncrossed her fingers as she left the girls' bathroom and headed back to the table. Now if Funny's parents said yes to her spending the night, she could do her second bit of spying. She could find out how a *chosen* child was treated, and then she'd know for sure just how unwanted she really was.

She noticed that the crowd at Bumpers was beginning to thin, but thankfully her friends and most of the cute boys were still there. She could see that Shane and Randy had gotten back to the table with their orders, and that Keith, Tony, and Jon had pulled up chairs and joined the group. Her friends seemed to have forgotten about the rotten mood she had been in lately, and her heart skipped a beat at the thought of all five of The Fabulous Five together with boyfriends. Rushing back to her friends, she was aware that everyone at the table was laughing.

"What's going on?" she asked.

"Didn't you hear?" cried Jana. "Tony found out that he isn't related to Sylvester Stallone after all. You know, the Italian Stallion."

"So, what's so funny about that?" asked Melanie.

"It's who he *is* related to that makes it funny," Katie insisted. "Madonna!"

"I still don't get it," said Melanie.

Finally Tony spoke up. "It's because she's a skinny girl and a singer instead of a macho-type guy," he said good-naturedly. "But she is *Italian*," he added, grinning broadly. "Her real name is Madonna Louise Veronica Ciccone, and we're umpteenth cousins twice removed on my mother's side."

"Well, at least she's famous," offered Melanie, and this time she joined in the laughter.

"Has anyone else found any famous relatives?" asked Christie. "Jana, what about Trevor Morgan?"

Jana shrugged. "I'm not sure. My Morgan relatives came from Manchester in England, which is where Trevor is from, but that's as much as I've been able to find out."

"Hey, you have to be related," shouted Keith. "How big a place can Manchester be?"

Jana shook her head. "It's a major city. It would be like saying we have to be related because both of our families came from Chicago or Boston."

"Well, keep digging," said Keith, giving her a grin.

"Let me tell you about my great-great-grandmother," Katie said proudly. "She worked for the passage of the Constitutional amendment in 1920 giving women the right to vote."

"*Aaaarrrrgghh*," groaned Tony, slapping his forehead. "We should have known."

Katie puffed out her chest and started to respond, but Melanie jumped into the conversation ahead of her. This was the moment she had been waiting for.

"I had a very interesting great-great-grandmother, too," she said, giving Shane a flirty smile. "Her name was Cordia Mae Lee, and I've been reading her love letters, which she kept tied with a pink ribbon. My grandmother keeps them in an old trunk at her house. All the boys were crazy about Cordia, and one even threatened to jump off the church steeple if she wouldn't go for a buggy ride with him."

Melanie looked at Shane again, hoping he would say something romantic, but instead it was Katie who spoke up again.

"Did you know that in the early 1800s only one letter in a hundred was addressed to a woman? Isn't that terrible? I read that in my genealogy research."

Leave it to Katie, Melanie thought, shaking her head.

After she and her friends left Bumpers, Melanie rushed home to wait for Funny's call. She had only been home a few minutes when the phone rang. It was Funny, saying that her parents had agreed to let Melanie spend the night.

"Actually they're awfully pleased," said Funny. "They said that they were glad I was expanding my circle of friends."

Melanie chewed her lower lip nervously when her parents dropped her off at Funny's house after dinner. They, too, had expressed approval that she was spending time with a new friend. If they only knew, she thought.

Mrs. Hawthorne answered the door. She was a tall woman with short, graying hair, and she was smiling so broadly that her face crinkled around her eyes. "Come on in, Melanie. We're so glad you'll be spending the night with us."

Just then Funny came bounding up, and her mother slipped an arm around her waist and went on talking. "Funny told us how you helped her overcome her shyness about talking to us about the genealogy project. We can't thank you enough."

Melanie nodded self-consciously and set her sleeping bag down on the floor. She could hardly stand to watch Funny and her mother hugging each other and smiling. It was happening just the way she had thought it would.

CHAPTER

12

"Come on up to my room," suggested Funny. She grabbed Melanie's sleeping bag and hoisted it onto her shoulder as she led the way up the stairs. Her bedroom was as cheerful as her disposition, with wallpaper made of happy faces of every color in the rainbow against a white background.

"Did you know I have a clown collection?" asked Funny, leading Melanie to a large glass-fronted cabinet containing clown dolls of every size and shape. "I've even thought about going to clown college myself one of these days," she admitted.

Melanie admired the clowns, and for the next

hour or so the two girls got settled and chatted about school and about boys.

"I get so embarrassed around boys that sometimes I'm even tongue-tied," said Funny. "I wish I could talk to them as easily as you can."

"What are you talking about?" Melanie asked, feeling a blush wash over her.

"It just seems to come so natural to you," Funny offered, and shrugged. "I couldn't help noticing you talking to Scott at the cemetery today, and then at Bumpers, Shane was hanging on every word you said."

"Oh, that," she said, feeling a tingling sense of pleasure. "Maybe I inherited it from one of my long-lost relatives," she joked.

"Maybe," Funny said, sounding doubtful. "Or maybe you just like to *flirt*." At that, both girls broke up laughing.

A little while later, they went down to the kitchen for a snack. Mrs. Hawthorne hummed softly as she tore lettuce leaves for a salad. She wore the same smile that had been on her face when Melanie arrived, and Melanie couldn't help thinking that Mrs. Hawthorne smiled as much as Funny did. Or was it the other way around? she wondered. Could Funny have gotten her smile from being around her adopted mother all the time? Mrs. Clark had said that everyone inherited traits from genes, but maybe Funny learned to be so smiley from being around Mrs. Hawthorne.

"This is usually Funny's job," Mrs. Hawthorne was saying. "But because she has company, I've given her the night off."

"Thanks, Mom," said Funny, giving her mother a look of genuine affection. Then laughing, she said, "I'll make *two* salads tomorrow night."

Melanie squirmed uncomfortably, trying to imagine her own mother taking over some of her chores just because she had company, but she couldn't. Of course, her company usually consisted of The Fabulous Five, whom her mother had known for years. But still, she thought, even if I brought home someone new, it probably wouldn't make any difference. I'm not a chosen child, like Funny. I'm an *accident*.

Later, when they went down to dinner, Funny ran squealing to her father, who had come home from work while they were upstairs, and he planted a kiss squarely on her forehead. "Hi, princess," he said, beaming down at her. "How was your day?"

Melanie thought about her own father the night before. Even though she had been home from school sick all day, he hadn't greeted her this way. All he had done was gripe about her table manners.

"Great," said Funny. "Today was our Family Liv-

ing class's field trip to the cemetery to make gravestone rubbings." She went on telling her parents
about the trip, and Melanie watched closely as they
listened to every word she said, just the way her own
parents had listened to Jeffy's story about the Godzilla movie the night before. But did my parents listen to me when I tried to tell them something? she
thought with a heavy heart. Of course not.

The rest of the evening went the same. Whenever
she and Funny were around Funny's parents, they
treated her as if she were some kind of royalty, and
Melanie felt herself growing quieter and quieter.

"Is something wrong?" Funny asked later when
they were snuggled in their sleeping bags and the
lights were turned out.

Melanie didn't say anything for a moment. How
could she tell Funny what was really bothering her?
She couldn't admit that the reason she had wanted to
spend the night was to spy on Funny and her family.

"There's nothing wrong," Melanie said at last.
"It's just that I can't help noticing how cheerful your
parents are."

"Yeah, I know what you mean." Funny giggled
softly in the dark. "My mom, especially. She can
always find something to smile about."

"Not *my* mom," grumbled Melanie. "Especially
where I'm concerned. All she ever does is yell at me."

Now it was Funny's turn to be silent, and Melanie

wished she could say more, but she could never tell
Funny the truth about what was bothering her.

A little while later, tiny, gurgly snores told
Melanie that Funny was asleep, but it was much
later before she was able to close her own eyes.

CHAPTER

13

*F*unny and her mother dropped Melanie off at home on their way to the library the next morning. Breakfast with the Hawthornes had been as cheerful as dinnertime had been the night before. Melanie moped around the house all morning, thinking about how Funny's parents treated their *chosen* child and wondering why she had spied on the Hawthornes in the first place. Because now that she had the proof she had been looking for, she felt worse instead of better.

She wished that she could talk to someone about her problem. She had tried to talk to The Fabulous Five at school the day before, but they had thought she was jumping to conclusions. "But they don't know how it feels," she whispered to herself.

She sat down at her desk and began to make a list of all the ways she could think of that her parents had proven over the last few days that they didn't love her. One, her mother hadn't been at home when she got sick and needed to come home. Of course, she had come straight to school and insisted that Melanie go home and then to bed once she had found out. But what else could a mother do?

"Melanie! Will you come down here right now and put your sleeping bag away!"

Melanie stiffened at her mother's angry voice. Big deal, she thought. Can't she ever give me a chance to do things on my own? I was going to put it away in a few minutes.

Putting down her ballpoint pen, she scuffed down to the foyer and scooped up the sleeping bag. Then she hauled it down to the basement and stuffed it into the closet.

The puppies were asleep in a furry pile. Rainbow was lying outside her box this time, and Melanie couldn't resist stopping to pet her.

"I'll bet you don't yell at your puppies the way my mom yells at me," she said, and chuckled.

Rainbow wagged her tail and gazed at Melanie lovingly. Giving her dog one last pat, she went back up to her room to work on her list again.

Two, her parents paid a lot more attention to Jeffy than they did to her. Of course she was older and needed some independence sometimes, but still . . .

"Melanie! You left the basement door open! Get down here this instant!"

Exasperated, Melanie sighed loudly. "Why doesn't she just close it herself?" she muttered out loud.

When she got to the kitchen, her mother was standing in the middle of the floor with her hands on her hips and an angry expression on her face.

Melanie opened her mouth to protest, but something caught her attention on the floor. Puddles. She gulped hard and began to count them. One. Two. Three. Four. Five. Six. Seven. Eight. Eight little puddles scattered all around the kitchen floor.

"Thanks to you," her mother went on, "the puppies got upstairs. I want this all cleaned up immediately."

Melanie nodded and went to get a bucket and a mop. There was no way she could argue this time. She was just finishing mopping the floor when the doorbell rang.

"I'll get it! I'll get it!" Jeffy screamed.

The next thing Melanie heard was Gran Pennington's cheerful voice. "Is Melanie here? I've brought something that I'm sure she'll want to see."

"In here, Gran," Melanie called. She put the mop in the bucket and turned to greet her grandmother.

"Oh, there you are," said Gran. She set her purse

on the counter and began rummaging through it. "I was thinking about your interest in your great-great-grandmother Cordia, and I remembered a newspaper clipping about her that I know you'll be interested in. I don't know why I forgot about it before, but luckily I found it in the trunk."

Beaming, she spread the old, yellowed newspaper clipping in front of Melanie. "My, my. You two are so much alike."

Melanie sucked in her breath. The headline read, "Courageous Girl Saves Doomed Dog From Certain Death." And there in the picture was Cordia Mae Lee, smiling and cuddling a brown and white dog.

"Read the story out loud," urged Gran Pennington.

Melanie cleared her throat and began, "'Thirteen-year-old Cordia Mae Lee, who lives on Brighton Street, was passing Thistle Creek yesterday when she heard a dog yelping. Upon investigation, she discovered that the dog had been thrown into the creek with a rock tied to its feet.' Oh, my gosh!" Melanie shrieked, and then read on quickly, "'Cordia jumped in and pulled the half-drowned dog out of the swift current, saving its life.'" Melanie glanced quickly from her grandmother to her mother and back to her grandmother again. "Why would anyone do something like that to a poor little dog?"

"That's one of the ways people used to get rid of

animals they didn't want in the days before there were animal shelters," her grandmother said gently. "But the important thing is that Cordia saved the little dog just as you and your friends saved all those animals at Christmastime. And she took it home to her family just as you brought Rainbow home. I guess you come by your love of animals naturally, don't you?"

Melanie swallowed back tears and nodded. It was too perfect to be true. She *had* really inherited a lot of things from this relative who had lived so long ago. If only she were alive today, she thought, we could be such good friends.

Gran Pennington let Melanie keep the clipping. And even though she read it over dozens of times over the rest of the weekend and smiled at the thoughts of all the things she had in common with her great-great-grandmother, she couldn't forget the problem that still nagged at her. She felt as unwanted as the two mutts, Rainbow and Cordia's little dog, had been.

When she got to school Monday morning, Melanie didn't feel like joining her friends at their usual spot by the fence, so she ambled over to a cluster of birch trees and stood by herself. She knew her rotten mood was back, and she didn't want to inflict it on The Fabulous Five.

"What's the matter, Mel?" Funny Hawthorne had walked up behind her and was looking at her with concern. "I can tell something is bothering you. It has been for days. I even noticed it when you spent the night with me Friday. Would you like to talk about it?"

Melanie felt tears jet into her eyes. "No," she whispered, looking away. "Thanks, though."

Funny didn't say anything for a moment as she drew circles into the dirt with the toe of her shoe. Finally she looked at Melanie and said, "I know how you feel. I didn't want to talk about my genealogy project last week either."

Melanie looked at her sharply. What does that have to do with anything? she wanted to ask.

"But you wouldn't leave me alone." A smile broke over Funny's face, and she went on, "You bugged me until I told you what the problem was. Remember?"

Melanie felt her face color as she nodded. Still, this was different. How could she talk about her own problem without letting Funny know that she was part of it?

"Soooo," Funny said, ignoring Melanie's silence, "I'm going to be just as good a friend to you as you were to me. I'm going to bug you. Come on, Melanie. You'll feel better when you talk about it, and maybe I can help."

Melanie looked at Funny as a tiny feeling of hope

rose in her. She really did need a friend. Maybe she could talk to Funny about part of her problem without telling her the whole story. "Remember how you thought you were a nobody in the Hawthorne family until you found out that you were chosen?"

"Sure," said Funny. "So what?"

Melanie took a deep breath and let it out in one big puff. "Well, it's just the opposite for me. I thought my parents really loved me until I read a letter my mom wrote to my grandmother saying that she and my dad never wanted me to be born."

Funny's eyes widened in disbelief as Melanie went on with her story, being careful to leave out the parts about her jealousy over Funny's being a chosen child. "You'd be in a bad mood, too, if you found out that you wrecked your mother's career and you were nothing but a burden to your family," Melanie blurted.

Funny looked down at the ground for a moment as if she were examining the circles in the dirt she had made with her toe a few moments before. Then she reached out a hand and touched Melanie softly on the arm. "I know all that seems awful right now, but I think you're wrong about not feeling wanted. Sure, your mom and dad yell at you sometimes, but everybody's mom and dad does that. Even mine," she said brightly. "They were just on good behavior because I had company when you were there."

"But I saw the proof," Melanie insisted, "right there in black and white in the letter. My mom said I was an accident!"

A determined look appeared on Funny's face. "Okay. Have it your way. Your parents hate you because you wrecked their life. But promise me you'll do exactly the same thing you made me do."

Melanie blinked, trying to remember their conversation a few days ago. "What was that?"

"Talk to your parents."

"What!" shrieked Melanie. "Are you kidding? I could never do a thing like that."

Funny smiled slyly. "That's what I said. Remember? And you convinced me that it was the only way to settle my problem and feel better about myself. If I could do it, *you can*."

"I don't know," said Melanie, shaking her head.

"You've got to promise," insisted Funny. "I'll throw my body across the door so that you can't get into school until you promise. I'll carry a sign that says 'Melanie Edwards is a chicken.' I'll drag you home and talk to your parents myself, if I have to."

Funny was saying all that in a teasing voice, but there was something about the look in her eyes that told Melanie she wasn't really kidding.

Melanie hesitated. Just because it had been the right thing for Funny didn't mean it would work for her. Still, something deep inside her was crying to be reassured that her parents loved her. "Okay," she murmured. "I guess I could try."

But Funny wouldn't let her off the hook yet. "Raise your right hand and swear," she ordered. "Swear you'll do it tonight."

Melanie couldn't help smiling at her determined friend as she raised her hand and swore to talk to her parents as soon as she got home from school. She was beginning to feel a little bit better already.

But when the bell sounded and she headed for her locker, her old doubts returned. Was it really the right thing to do or would it only make things worse?

CHAPTER

14

*M*elanie's heart was throbbing in her ears when she went down to dinner that night. She had changed her mind about talking to her parents at least a hundred times during the day. One moment she would be determined to find out the truth from them, even if it meant hearing proof that they didn't love her. The next moment she would chicken out, deciding that she couldn't really face it. Finally she made up her mind to do it, but she planned to wait until dinner so that she could speak to both of them at once. She knew Jeffy would be there, too, and would overhear everything, but it was just a chance she would have to take.

111

Melanie waited until the food had been passed around the table to bring up what was on her mind.

"Mom. Dad," she began. "Remember when I told you about going to Gran Pennington's and reading a stack of love letters written to Great-great-grand-mother Cordia?"

Her father chuckled. "See, what did I tell you? She was a real corker, wasn't she? Had young men falling all over themselves for her attention."

Melanie nodded. "Well, that's not the only letter I read. I read the one you wrote to Gran to tell her you were going to have me."

She waited a moment to see if either of them would react with horror at the possibility that their secret was out, but nothing like that happened. Instead, her mother smiled happily and said, "Boy, that was a long time ago."

Suddenly all the anxiety Melanie had felt before engulfed her and she choked back tears to blurt out, "It said that . . . that I wrecked your chances for a career, Mom, and that I was just an *accident*!"

All action at the table stopped, except for Jeffy, who was picking pieces of rice off his plate with his fingers, and both her mother and her father stared at her in astonishment.

"What are you talking about?" whispered her mother.

"That you didn't want me then and you don't now. That's the truth, isn't it?"

Mr. and Mrs. Edwards exchanged glances. "Tell us what the letter said," her father asked gently.

Melanie closed her eyes. She could see the words as clearly as if they were written on the insides of her eyelids. "It said, 'Larry and I had planned to wait awhile to have a baby,'" she recited. "'You know how I've worked for years to become a concert pianist and have given up a lot to achieve my dream. But accidents happen, I guess, and now I'll have to forget that dream . . .'" Her words trailed off, and she felt as if she were collapsing from the weight of her heart.

"Go on," her mother urged.

Melanie looked at her blankly.

"That's not all it said," Mrs. Edwards prompted. "I remember that letter as if I wrote it yesterday."

"But I didn't read any more," Melanie admitted bitterly. "I didn't need to. I already knew the truth."

"Oh, sweetheart!" cried her mother. She got up from her place at the table and rushed to Melanie, gathering her in her arms. "There's so much more. Come on. Get your coat. We'd better go to Gran Pennington's right now so that you can read the rest."

To Melanie's astonishment her parents got up from the table even though their meal was barely touched. They dressed Jeffy in his snowsuit, handed him a cookie, and then got their own coats. Melanie followed them like a sleepwalker. Nothing seemed real, and even though her mother had said that there was more to the letter, she couldn't forget the words she had already seen.

Gran Pennington was surprised to see them when she opened the door, but Melanie's mother said something to her in low tones, and Gran nodded and led them upstairs to the room where the trunk stood. Melanie stared at the trunk and the old feelings of indecision came back. She wanted to see the letter, especially if she had missed something important. But at the same time, she was afraid.

"Would you like for me to get the letter out for you?" Gran Pennington asked gently.

Mealnie shook her head. "That's okay," she said. "I'll get it."

She knelt beside the trunk and slowly lifted the lid. The same musty smell floated toward her as before, and the stack of letters tied neatly with a pink ribbon were exactly where she had left them. Taking a deep breath, she carefully extracted the letter from under them and held it up.

"Go ahead," her mother urged. "Read *all* of it."

Slowly Melanie pulled the sheets of paper out of the envelope. She swallowed hard and began to read.

Dear Mom,

I know you've been wondering why I haven't written in such a long time and that you always say that no news is good news, but the truth is, I haven't been sure if the news I'm going to tell you is good news or not.

Larry and I had planned to wait awhile to have a baby. You know how I've worked for years to become a concert pianist and have given up a lot to achieve my dream. But accidents happen, I guess, and now I'll have to forget that dream.

The first page ended there, and Melanie took a deep breath and began reading page two.

And yet, Larry and I have begun looking at it another way. Even though the old dreams may be lost, at least for now, we have a new and more wonderful dream to take its place. A baby to care for and to love. Who knows how long it might have been before we would have known this happiness if things had gone the way we'd planned. So I guess I have to say that this accident was really a blessing in disguise.

> *Love,*
> *Kathy*

Slowly Melanie raised her eyes and looked first at her mother and then her father. "A blessing?" she whispered around the lump in her throat.

"That's right," said her mother. "We've always loved you and we always will."

Dropping the letter, Melanie rushed to them for the best hug of her life.

In bed that night, Melanie waited until the house was quiet. Then she got up and tiptoed to her desk, getting Great-great-grandmother Cordia's photograph album off her desk and bringing it back to bed. She got the flashlight out of the drawer in her bedside table and pulled the covers over her head the way she used to do when she was small. She wasn't hiding from her parents this time. She just felt more private this way.

For the next few minutes she looked at the pictures of her great-great-grandmother, tingling with pleasure when she thought about all they had in common. She was glad that the Family Living classes had started the genealogy project because she had learned some valuable things. She knew now that even though Funny was adopted, her cheerful personality came from the Hawthorne family, and that she had gotten her sunny smile from Mrs. Hawthorne even though they weren't related by blood.

I've learned that my parents really do love me, she thought, no matter how grouchy they get sometimes or how much Mom yells at me. My friends in The

Fabulous Five were right when they thought I was jumping to conclusions.

She smiled down at Cordia's face in the picture, feeling for the hundredth time that she was looking into a mirror. And I've learned that some things can be passed down through the generations. Snapping off the flashlight, she lay back on her pillow and began to make plans. First, she would look at every single thing in the trunk to find out as much as she could about Cordia. Surely there would be something in there telling whom she married. Maybe then I'll know whom I'll marry someday, too.

But for now, there were other things to do. Romantic things that she had never thought of before. The next time Scott came over, she would invite him into the backyard and ask him to push her on Jeffy's swing. Then, when it snowed again, she'd coax Shane into making a snowman with her.

"Oooooh," she whispered as she drifted off to sleep, "I guess I just can't help being a flirt."

CHAPTER

15

*C*urtis Trowbridge walked into Christie Winchell's homeroom class with his usual air of importance. Besides being class president, he was also seventh-grade editor for the school newspaper, *The Smoke Signal*. He obviously felt it was an honor to deliver personally the latest edition to the homerooms.

"Thank you, Curtis," said Mr. Neal. "Heather, would you and Bill Soliday pass out *The Smoke Signal*, please?"

Christie looked at her watch. There were still ten minutes before the bell, and she had all her homework done, so she could spend the rest of the period reading the paper. It was fun to search through it to

119

see if any of The Fabulous Five's names or the names of the boys they hung out with were in it. She scanned the pages, finding several boys she knew in articles on the sports pages and Beth Barry's name in a story about the drama club.

As she turned the newspaper back over to the front page, an article there caught her eye.

> *Homework Hot-Line to Be Established*
> *It was announced today by Mr. Bell that Wakeman Junior High is going to establish a Hot-Line Center so that students may call in at night and get help with their homework. The center will have special telephone numbers and operate from seven to nine each evening, Monday through Thursday. Several students from the seventh, eighth, and ninth grades who have nothing lower than a B in any class will be asked to man the center.*

I'll probably get asked, thought Christie. After all, I made all A's in my first semester at Wacko. It sounds like fun, and who knows, while I'm helping other kids I might even meet a cute boy.

But Christie encounters more than she expects when she joins the Hot-Line Center and tries to track down a mysterious caller before he does something terrible. Join Christie as she uses all her brains and courage in her search for clues to the caller's identity in *The Fabulous Five #16: The Hot-Line Emergency.*

ABOUT THE AUTHOR

Betsy Haynes, the daughter of a former news-woman, began scribbling poetry and short stories as soon as she learned to write. A serious writing career, however, had to wait until after her marriage and the arrival of her two children. But that early practice must have paid off, for within three months Mrs. Haynes had sold her first story. In addition to a number of magazine short stories and the Taffy Sinclair series, Mrs. Haynes is also the author of *The Great Mom Swap* and its sequel, *The Great Boyfriend Trap*. She lives in Colleyville, Texas, with her husband, who is also an author.